LEIF'S JOURNEY

Leif's Journey

Terry Hokenson

namelos
South Hampton, New Hampshire

Library of Congress Control Number: 2014944860

ISBN 978-1-60898-183-0 (hardcover: alk. paper)
ISBN 978-1-60898-184-7 (paperback: alk. paper)
ISBN 978-1-60898-185-4 (ebook)

www.namelos.com

To my brothers

CHAPTER 1

Upsala, Minnesota, January 1881

"I will go, Pa."

Leif scraped the last oatmeal out of his bowl with a spoon he'd carved from a block of ash.

"Jag ska gå, far."

He said it in a flat tone, as if he would go simply out of duty. Or as if he thought nothing of it. But inside, he was doing handsprings. He would go to Freeport on his own. Never mind the worst snowstorms anybody could remember.

He was ready for anything. Anything to break the monotony. The farm got mighty close in the dead of winter. Especially this winter. Leif escaped any way he could. A few weeks ago he'd gone to the old log toolshed, cleared the chimney of bird nests, and lighted a fire. But too much of the chinking between the logs had fallen out, and the place wouldn't hold heat. He also went out to check his snares every other day and sometimes brought back a snowshoe hare or two for dinner.

Another time he carved a shelter in a snowbank down by the creek and sat on some hides for a spell, wondering what the rest of the world was like. All he knew of the world beyond his home came from reading the Little Falls newspaper, hearing people talk, and a trip to Freeport a couple years ago.

He'd read everything in the house at least twice. Jules Verne was his favorite. And he loved Daniel Defoe's *Robinson Crusoe*. He even kept a diary in a bound record book that his sister, Ellen, had sent him from Minneapolis. On the third page he'd written, "I sharpened a chisel, a couple scythes, and two knives for Mr. Harjie, and he told me I was the best blade dresser in all of Morrison County. I wish he would tell Pa."

Keeping the leather goods—the harnesses and traces—in good repair was Pa's domain. So were the family shoes and the tool belts. He worked in the tack room in the corner of the barn where there was a small woodstove. Not much Leif had to do in the barn, just tend to the few animals they kept—three cows, four horses, six sheep, two goats, and the chickens. Ya, there was Horace, too, but he was practically human. He was Leif's pet for life.

"Horace," Leif had said when he'd gone out to the barn before breakfast, "I've got some excellent fare for you today." Leif poured the kitchen slop pail into the elderly pig's trough. Leif made some such pompous announcement every day, but Horace ignored them. After nearly thirteen years of friendship with Leif, the pig really didn't feel the need to comment much. A wag of his sprightly tail and a few grunts usually sufficed.

"*Hnnhh, hnhh*," Horace murmured as he sniffed the offerings, which included a few overripe potatoes, some scorched corn pancakes, and the contents of a jar of stewed tomatoes that Ma said smelled off. Leif always mixed in some corn and oats, too. Horace loved bones and gristle, but when the family ate pork, Leif would pull the bones and gristle out of the slop for the sake of decency.

While Horace enjoyed his meal, Leif cleaned his pen and laid down some fresh straw for him. "My friend, before long we are all going to be living under one big snowdrift." Horace looked up and eyeballed Leif. Slop ran down the pig's chin. "All right, I'm exaggerating," said Leif.

In the winter Horace got an extra portion of straw and an old horse blanket. He'd taken to snuggling with the goats when it got really cold. One night the mercury fell into the thirties below zero. Leif looked in on him and found him sleeping soundly with the other animals.

Everybody had a lot to do except in the pit of winter when, for days on end, you had to make up things to keep busy. Leif liked to carve wood or beeswax or soap. He might chitchat with Ma if he were so inclined. Or not. Pa didn't generally go in for chitchat unless you asked for advice. And then he might just answer you with one word or a grunt.

And as for whittling, how many wooden spoons could they use? He had been carving chains, even flowers, to decorate the walls.

Just the three of them now, since the hired man had left after the harvest.

Freeport! Could be a three-day trip with all the snow. Supply wagons had been stopped now for nearly two months. How poor his oatmeal tasted without cinnamon. Drifts came halfway up the first-floor windows on the west side. Pa'd said it was the hardest winter yet since they'd come to Upsala. That was eighteen years ago.

Leif drank down the last of his coffee.

He had to get ready. Plan it out—which way he would go, what he would take, what he had to do. Leif balanced his spoon in his fingers, elbows on the table. When he carved a spoon, he liked to make a thick handle so that it was easy to get a good grip.

Bjorn, his Pa, spat into the spit mug that he used for chaw. He was always the first one done eating.

"I'll take the Springfield, then," said Leif.

"Nay," grunted his father. "*Ta Vinchestern.*" His steel gray eyes reminded Leif of the cloudy-moon eyes of a walleye. The eyes of a cold-blooded creature. Leif had taken after his mother—brown eyes and hair near as dark as a bear's fur.

Leif nodded. "Ya, that's good. I'll take the Winchester, Pa."

The Winchester! That's what he really wanted to take. It was a much better rifle. The Springfield was an old military gun that was ready to fall apart. You couldn't hit the barn with it at thirty yards.

But with Pa you had to use strategy. He was contrary. Pa might have told him to take the Winchester just because Leif had offered to take the Springfield. You didn't talk back to Pa—not unless you wanted him to smack you with the back of his hand.

Truth be told, Pa had never smacked Leif in the face with the back of his hand. He had threatened to do it; he'd drawn his hand back. But he never had hit Leif in the face. Leif had seen him backhand his older brothers, though. He looked at the sitting room's golden yellow wallpaper covered with tiny bouquets. That was where he'd seen Pa smack Elias just before Elias left home. Ya, Elias declared he would leave, and he did.

Pa would shove Leif in the shoulder, grab his arm once in a while. But he'd never backhanded him across the face. Leif figured it was because of the accident, when he fell from the wagon. At the age of four he'd fallen out while Pa was driving very fast, and the rear wheel had sliced a fearful wound in the top of Leif"s head.

"Wash your dishes while the water's hot, Leif," said his mother, Birke. She put the kettle back on the cast iron stove. Leif picked up his bowl and spoon and moved to the sink.

In summer, riding horses to Freeport from Upsala through the heavy woods and thick prairie grass took a day and a half. He'd gone there with his brother Rollie once. There were bridges, two of them—one over the river and one across a creek. The wagon track was half hidden in grass for most stretches. If you were walking, you could save time by crossing hummocks and dips that the wagons went around. Most of them. A few were boggy traps.

With the deep snow, and on foot, it would surely take double the time or more. Leif dried his bowl and spoon and put them on the shelf.

The snow was far too deep for a sleigh. A horse would have a devil of a time moving through it just by himself, let alone carrying a load. Most likely couldn't even do it more than a few yards. Deer get trapped in deep snow sometimes. They thrash around and make a pit and then lie low.

Of course the wolves look for them.

Belka yipped outside the door. Leif took a bone from the slop bucket under the sink and tossed it out to him.

Five or six feet of snow smothered the countryside. A grain wagon could be totally buried.

The horses had to stay in the barn. You could shovel away the snow and open the barn doors, but they couldn't go anywhere except to follow the slot to the house or to the toolshed, and they didn't like to get in those narrow chutes. Except Star, who would come to the house for a carrot.

Leif would walk in the Indian snowshoes and pull the toboggan behind him.

"Would you take the drain water out, then?" asked Ma. Leif took the wooden pail from under the sink, paused to pull his cap over his head, and went out the door quickly, drawing it shut behind him. The air was crackling cold, with the barest breeze.

He went around behind the farmhouse, his boots squeaking in the snow, and dumped the bucket in a nest of dirty straw.

The snow along the path was nearly five feet deep. He walked in the trench, looked out across the crystalline dunes. Soon to set in the west, the moon shone like a fisheye through a haze of fine, blowing snow. In the bone-bare aspen grove lay a hill of snow covering a sod mound that was once the family's potato keep and before that, for seven months, long ago, it was home. Newcomer Bjorn Eliasson had quickly built a small log house and put a cedar-shake roof on it. That house was now the toolshed. Its weathered wood shone silver and black.

The moonlight cast a faint green-and-red glow on the snow, and Leif's breath made pale rainbow smoke in the early light. He had skied to the willow on Crane Creek yesterday and looked upon the snow snaking away to the southeast. It meandered along the bottom where the creek ran on its way to the Elmdale River. Someday he'd like to take a boat and go all the way to the Mississippi.

In Freeport he would get the flour, chaw tobacco for Pa, coffee and sundries for Ma—including cinnamon, he hoped. The flour would come in a fifty-pound sack, enough for another couple months. Maybe by April the supply wagons would make it out to the Upsala store again. That's what Pa thought. "The good Lord willing," said Ma.

The cold was now burning through his shirt and wool union suit and sinking its numbing little needles into his chin and fingers. He walked back. When he opened the door, a white cloud spilled out and boiled away in the cold. He closed the door quickly behind him and set the pail back under the sink. "I'll take the toboggan," he said as he hung his fur cap back on its peg by the door.

"Eh?" grunted Pa, arching his juniper-bush eyebrows. His question crouched on its belly like a badger. You didn't know which way it was going to spring. Why had he mentioned it? The less said, the better.

Leif was not built like a bear, as Pa was. Surely Pa could see that. Even if it were summer, Leif would need a horse to carry a fifty-pound sack, and now everywhere lay more than five feet of snow.

Leif weighed barely a hundred and thirty pounds. At seventeen, he was like an outsized coyote.

Pa gave him a testy look. Leif studied the feathery patterns in the frost on the window over the sink. Pa made out like Leif was lazy, always trying to take the easy way. In truth Leif was long used to scything hay all day and plowing the fields until the horses had to rest. Strong, sure—but lean as a coyote.

"I'm not raising no sissies," Pa muttered in English, as if that were the language of doubtful characters.

"Ya, Pa, that's a fact." Leif's neck burned at his father's scorn. Pa's arm flinched as if he'd thought to give Leif the back of his hand but wasn't sure if he'd been sassed or not. Pa turned away and spat again into his black mug.

Sometimes it seemed as if it wasn't really him his father was talking to. He'd talked the same way to Rollie and Elias.

Leif grabbed his cap and stepped outside again. He looked toward the round disk of the early morning sun, just above the horizon in the southeast, glowing red as it rose behind the cloud bank. Pa tore down everything he said or did. "I'm seventeen," he said to himself. "I do a man's work. Gordon Harjie praised the way I sharpened his scythe and knife blades. Pa always finds some fault, and then he mocks me: 'Who taught you to walk like that?' 'Where did you learn to hold the gun like that?'" He spat bitterly into the snow. Pa showed more respect to strangers. A knot formed in his throat.

"Nothing I do is ever good enough for him. He pretends I'm useless, but now that Rollie and Elias are gone, I do the lion's share of the work. Of course, that's expected. You get no credit for doing what's expected." Leif clenched his teeth and squeezed his fists in his pockets.

He knew that he stood to take over the farm. But living under Pa's hand was a heavy price to pay. Maybe he, too, would go away. His breath boiled up in clouds that hung around his head. The cold pinched his nose and chin. Jumpin' Jehoshaphat. It must be twenty below. He went back inside, pulled on coat and mitts, and stepped out on the porch again. Belka ran up to him wagging his whole rear end, wanting to play—and get more to eat. His caramel-colored winter fur was thick and carried a few straws from his bedding in the barn.

Leif grabbed Belka's head in both hands. He pounced on the dog and rolled in the snow with him, growling like a bear. Belka easily slipped out of his arms, barking happily. "All right, then, I'll get you another bone," said Leif.

Many times they had shoveled the porch to keep it clear around the door. But snow had piled high all around, and blew back down. Just as often the pit had to be cleared in front of the steps. Anyone who arrived descended into it before stepping onto the porch and from it led the slot to the barn.

Belka was a shepherd, born to herd sheep. He tried to herd the chickens. Of course, that's like trying to eat soup with one finger. Once Belka brought a deer to him, but Leif didn't shoot for fear he might hit the dog by accident.

Leif pulled the toboggan out of the snowdrift by the tool-shed. Every time he looked at the log shed, he marveled that the family of six had fit inside. It was the place where he'd been born.

He knocked the snow off the toboggan with his mitt. He would leave the next morning just before dawn. The moon would be over half full, plenty bright to see by with all the snow reflecting the light. He would wear his wool jacket, tightly woven on a loom by Ma's ma, and an old gabardine vest that he had lined with rabbit furs. And of course his prized hooded buffalo robe.

For the robe he had traded an anvil that he'd found at a ruined farmstead. Naturally, Pa had scorned his bargain. "Det envil was worth three of dem robes," he'd snorted. But they already had an anvil, and the robe was a fine one, thick and supple. Leif also had thick sheepskin mitts and a winter cap he'd sewn from raccoon skins. Ellen had showed him how to make the stitches. He missed his older sister.

That night Leif could hardly get to sleep. Freeport was a good twenty miles across country. Much of the way lay through thick woods, and you had to mark trees with an ax so you could find your way back. In a winter like this, it was not a trip for a fool. It would be a great adventure!

When he woke, it was still dark. The kitchen stove crackled and clicked downstairs as Ma loaded wood and swung the iron door shut. He woke again a few minutes later to the smell of woodsmoke. He slipped out from under the warm wool quilts and dressed quickly.

When it was twenty or thirty below, he wore a woolen union suit, thick socks and a stocking cap to bed. When it was that cold, he didn't waste time while putting his clothes on in the morning.

While Ma heated water, Leif went out to the barn and took care of Horace and the animals, milked the cows, and brought the pails of milk back to the house. He was all packed and ready to go.

Pa had gone into the workroom at the back of the barn to start the woodstove. He'd spend the day mending harnesses and sharpening tools or whatever he could find to do.

Leif ate his oatmeal porridge, thinking about the route he would take, while Ma made bread dough. "Tie Belka up in the barn, so he don't follow you," said Ma.

"He'll stay if I tell him to."

"Leif," Ma said quietly. Leif looked up at her. "You get to Freeport," she said, "go to the root lady, Miz Charbonnier, and tell her your ma needs a remedy."

"Ya," said Leif, eyes round.

"Tell her she got pain under the bottom rib on the right side, close to the center. Pull up your shirt." Leif pulled up his shirt. "In here," Birke said, "put your fingers there." Leif did as he was told. "The pain takes my breath away, tell her. It's worst when—" She looked straight into Leif's eyes and mouthed the words, "—when your Pa's . . . in a temper." Leif nodded.

"I know, Ma." The yelling and ranting, the cursing and the long silences. That they all knew. Ma looked away.

"All right, Ma," said Leif. Those times when Pa was raging, they found other things to do, like take the boat down the creek to fish or go weed the garden.

"Where do I find her? The root lady."

"Ask in town," said Ma. "West of the village somewhere. Leif?"

"Yes, Ma?"

"Take this and offer it to her." Ma handed Leif a small black velvet bag with a soft yellow drawstring. Leif hefted it and looked inside. He drew a sharp breath and frowned.

"Ma! No! You must keep this!" It was her own mother's wedding ring.

"Leif, it's very important. You must offer it to her." Her brown eyes shone out of dark circles.

Pa stepped in the door, hung his coat and cap on a peg, and sat down for breakfast.

Leif lashed his rucksack of gear and supplies to the toboggan on top of the hides—deer, raccoon, muskrat. Selling some hides now and then was one of the few ways he had to earn a little spending money. In the sack he had stowed a pot, a hunting knife wrapped in a rag, a pewter mug, and a thick wool sweater to sleep in. Pa had handed him a heavy wool horse blanket, neatly rolled. He also carried an ax, a bundle of Swedish safety matches, three beeswax candles, a small clay lamp that burned fat, and a block of frozen lard. And of course the Winchester.

Pa came out of the house and stood in his wool shirt, suspenders, and canvas pants, with his hair and beard awry. He picked up the short-handled scoop shovel he'd left leaning next to the door.

"You better take dis."

"Ya. Good," said Leif. Pa handed him the shovel. Leif tied it down. Ma came out with a small cloth sack. Pulling her coat close around her neck, she tipped her head, giving him a tight smile. Pa pursed his lips; then the furrow appeared between his brows, and he looked away toward Freeport. He set his jaw and did not look Leif in the face.

Ma handed him the bag. "Until you shoot something for dinner."

He looked into the bag, gave Ma a wink and a grin, and stuffed it into the sling pouch inside his coat. In the bag were dried apples, hardtack, and venison jerky. But their stores were getting low. He would need to shoot some game. He would have to move quietly, like a coyote, through the snow-burdened woods and meadows.

"You got de money, den?" said Pa.

"Ya," said Leif, clapping his mitt to his chest. Ma had folded the three one-dollar bills neatly and pinned them inside his shirt pocket. It was a lot of money. He bent over and tied the lampwick bindings of the Indian snowshoes around his boots.

Ma stepped forward, and he gave her a hug; then he shook Pa's hand. Pa's hands were huge, and rough as bark, but he never squeezed hard in a handshake. He looked down when he shook Leif's hand, stuck out his chin, and nodded.

Leif picked up the towline of the toboggan and walked away toward the southwest. Belka barked once from the tack room in the barn. After fifty paces he turned and waved. His mother waved back. Pa had already gone inside.

Leif turned and followed Crane Creek to the south. His snowshoes sank eight or ten inches deep with each step in the plush new snow.

When he had walked perhaps an hour, far from the fretful farmhouse, long after the creek had wandered eastward again, he stopped and looked around. Meadow and forest swelled with drifts. Thor had surely seized the earth for a winter of the gods. Out of the darkness of the woods he saw a barred owl swoop silently down to the snow and pluck up a small creature in its talons.

Leif took the rifle out of its canvas bag and stood still upon the snowshoes, searching the naked birch and aspen and the deep green spruces in their shawls of snow. A few crows cried out, piercing the cold wild air.

In winters past Pa used to go off to work in the logging camps up north, and he'd be gone for weeks. Elias and Rollie would boss Leif around and torment him until Ellen or his mother stepped in. Then they taunted him as "Mama's boy." But when Elias left for Dakota and Rollie headed off for Oregon, Leif was lost. Ellen had moved to Minneapolis five years earlier. Leif was left alone.

He knew why his sister and his two brothers had left: freedom. He wanted that freedom. Freedom to do what he wanted without Pa constantly ordering him to do this, do that, fetch this, fetch that. "Where you get dat idea? Do you tink I'm stupid?" And "Why did you do dat, you idiot! You want me to get de strap?" Or "No, you don't need dat. No, you can't go dere." And "Don't sass me, boy, or I'll give you de back of my hand." Always criticism and threats; never praise, never thanks, never trust.

He walked on. Maybe he would soon go off, too, and try his luck. Then who would take over the farm? It might go to strangers who wouldn't know what the heap of sod in the aspens was or the log toolshed where he had been born. They'd know nothing of the dreams he had dreamed in the arms of the willow on the creek.

Maybe he would stay. If any of them could manage it, Ellen had said, it would be him. Leif didn't know. He couldn't figure out why she would say that.

It was true that he got away with talking back to Pa more than anybody. But he was always that way. Ellen said he had learned bad habits while he was being nursed back from death's doorstep after he'd gotten his head sliced.

Pa had been gentle with him. After he'd lain in bed a few days with an herbal poultice on his wound, Pa came and squatted down beside the bed. "You want to go outside, boy?" Pa turned, Leif crawled upon his back, and Pa carried him outside. Leif asked to be put down. He walked, but he got dizzy and sat down on the grass. Pa then picked him up and took him back to the house. He rested his hot face in Pa's beard, and Pa hummed a tune.

During the second week one evening after supper, when Pa spoke a few words about the day's events with Ma, Leif went to him and sought to crawl into his lap. He permitted this two or three times, but then he told Leif that it was time he sat in his own chair. If he was tired, he should go to bed. The comfort time with Pa came to an end.

When he'd started walking around again, Ma had woven him a helmet of slender willow laces that resembled a bird's nest. She lined it with flannel, and she made him wear it whenever he wasn't in bed. He was warned not to run for fear of falling down. But eventually the fire on his head went out, and no one could keep him from running.

About that time Ma brought him a baby pig. "He's sick, Leif, so you need to feed him with this bottle like a baby and keep checking on him." Leif took to the task with solemn relish. For years they thought he'd named the pig Horse. But when he saw the name Horace in the newspaper at the age of ten, he knew that was his friend's true name.

Yes, the comfort time came to an end a long time ago. But Leif still spoke his mind to Pa now and then.

CHAPTER 2

A Chance Encounter

Out of the corner of his eye Leif saw movement to the left. It was a deer. It stood upwind of him at the edge of thick brush. Slowly, like the minute hand of a clock, Leif began raising the Winchester and turning toward the deer. He was holding the toboggan's towline but couldn't drop it for fear of spooking the animal. He turned—slowly, slowly—bringing the rifle up. He pulled the trigger. *Click.* The deer slipped back into the brush. He'd forgotten to load shells in the magazine. He loaded five shells and began walking again.

"Idiot!" he said to himself.

"Eh, why talk to myself like Pa? It's not safe to put a gun away loaded. I just forgot." Leif had brought down many a squirrel, many a rabbit and pheasant with that rifle, an 1873 Winchester model 44-40 that Pa had taken in trade for repairing some machinery.

Leif had gotten meat for the table since he was six years old. In those days he had taken a stout stick and gone out with old Tryg. The dog would sight a rabbit and feign attack to keep it distracted while Leif sneaked up on it and—*thump!*—another rabbit to skin and clean for dinner.

Ma, Pa, Ellen, and his brothers had come over from Sweden, the old country across the ocean that Leif knew little about. Pa never spoke of it, but he still tapped his foot, wore half a smile, and got a tear in his eye when the old timers played folk tunes on the accordion and the fiddle. And if he'd had a few mugs of beer, he'd grab Ma and join the dancers. When Leif was young, Pa and Ma would dance as long as the music played. Pa's knees weren't so bad then.

Leif checked his old brass compass and walked on, getting hungry, looking out for something to shoot. He took the last drink of water from the leather canteen that he carried inside his vest. Another hour passed, and he gnawed on a piece of hardtack. The thick, dense biscuits were so tough, he had to break off a piece in his teeth and suck on it for a while before he could chew it. The sky had turned gray and heavy. Snow fell faster by the minute.

Wait. Something was moving. Not like an animal. Like a human.

"Hullo!" Leif called through the heavy haze of falling snow. Something or somebody was straggling in the drifts off to the left. The movements were slow and lurching. It could be a deer, perhaps. But it hadn't been spooked by his call. Leif walked toward the figure and called again, "Hullo!" The figure stopped. "Hullo!" came a female voice.

Leif paced toward her and called, "Hullo, neighbor!"

The voice called back, "Ya!"

He walked toward her and called out, "Hullo! I'm Leif Eliasson, from Upsala!" She looked at him warily, clutching her hood at the neck against the gusts of wind.

"Are you all right?" Leif asked.

"Oh, ya," she said as Leif came within a few yards of her.

She looked frightened. She was wearing skis, but she had no poles. Strange.

"Don't worry. I mean no harm," said Leif. "Are you all right? What brings you out here?" She opened her mouth to speak, but nothing came out.

"You have trouble?" Leif asked.

"A little, ya," she said, looking behind her.

"Don't worry," said Leif. "How can I help you?" She was shaking—whether from cold or fright, he could not tell. She had her arms crossed, her hands tucked underneath them.

"My uncle, he chased me out. I am heading for the Westrich farm!" she said. Leif looked around. It was late. Darkness had begun to settle in. Falling snow had brought the light down, too.

"He chased you away from home?" Leif asked. She nodded and looked back in the direction she'd come, clutching her hooded jersey at the throat. She looked at him.

"My parents left yesterday . . . to meet the new preacher at the neighbors' . . . and while they were gone . . . my crazy uncle Henrik came, and . . . I had to run away from him." She was breathing in bursts. "I had to put on this old woolen jersey—couldn't even get my winter coat! I had to use these old skis from the barn, with a bad binding on one and no poles. It's another four miles to the Westrich farm!" She threw up her arms and dropped them.

Leif ejected the remaining shells from the Winchester, put them in his coat pocket, and slipped the rifle into its canvas case. This was strange!

"It's getting dark," he said. He looked off to the west. "Four miles." He looked down and then turned to the girl, shaking his head.

"Too far. Snow's getting bad, and the wind is rising. How far is your house?" He tied the rifle on the toboggan.

"It's across the lake about two miles," the girl said, looking back.

"By the way, my name is Leif."

"Ya, so you said. I'm Anna. My parents are Alder and Gaia Sederstrom." She looked and sounded close to Leif's age.

"I'm on my way to Freeport," he said. Helping Anna return to the farmstead seemed out of the question.

"It's going to be dark soon. We need to take shelter," said Leif. "Looks like another blizzard." The snow was now driving down in blankets, muffling sight and sound.

"Ya," said Anna, clutching her hood around her face. "It is. So what's your plan?"

"I just passed by some big spruces back there," Leif said, gesturing into the haze. "We can take shelter under one of them."

He pulled the toboggan around. "Here," Leif said, "get on if you like. Go ahead."

"I'll just ski, thank you."

"All right." Leif turned with the toboggan back toward the spruces, and Anna paced alongside in the heavy old sliders. Though he could not see the spruces yet, he could see his own tracks and follow them back.

Leif soon came upon the dark bulk of the spruces. "All right," he said, puffing, already half-covered with snow. "I'll get the shovel out." He untied it from the toboggan. Anna, also cloaked in snow, squatted down while Leif untied the scoop shovel. He looked frankly at her. She huddled beside the toboggan, holding her hood closed around her face while the wind whipped snow around them.

"I have a blanket," said Leif, thrusting the shovel upright in the snow. He opened the rucksack on the toboggan, took out the horse blanket and unrolled it. "Here, you can wrap yourself up." She took the flapping blanket.

"*Tack*—thank you. This old jersey doesn't cut the wind much," said Anna as she sat down on the toboggan and drew the blanket around her in the swirling snowfall. "I can dig, too, if you get tired," she called.

Leif excavated a trench in the snow down toward the base of the tree. The snow there was already close to five feet deep, and as he made his way down between the lower branches into the hollow under the tree, he scooped away the drift and cleared an area on the ground down to a thick mat of needles. The spruce's natural shape had already fended off a lot of snow. Underneath there was not much to remove.

Leif carried a scoop full of snow up the trench and threw it aside. A girl! Leif's heart pounded, and his thoughts whirled as he worked. He would have to dig two shelters. Within fifteen minutes he had prepared an entry leading down under the spruce. He went up to Anna.

"It's ready," he said. "Go ahead, crawl in." Anna stepped out of the skis and planted them upright in the snow. She crouched down and descended into the dark cavern under the branches, taking the blanket with her. Leif followed her. "To the left. You can go in there." Anna crawled into the hollow, shook the snow off herself, wrapped up in the blanket, and sat down.

"I will make room for myself on the other side here," said Leif. The spruce was a large one—maybe sixteen feet across at the base. Its downward-spreading branches shed the snow and kept the space under the tree clear while the snow built up a wall all around. The lower branches made a ceiling about two feet off the ground. It would be fine.

Leif brought the rest of his gear down and propped the

toboggan up to close the hole. The tree was completely muffled in snow. A cone of gray silence filled with black branches rose above them, a webwork of chimneys leading nowhere. Leif could just make out Anna's form only a few feet from him.

"You might like to lie on top of these hides."

"All right." Anna raised herself up as he slid them underneath her. Though they were stiff as platters, they were furry proof against the frozen ground.

"Good. They cut off the cold underneath," she said. The tree creaked slightly, and bits of snow floated down.

"The wind is blowing hard now," said Leif. "Are you all right?"

"Yes, I'm much warmer," said Anna. "It's good to be out of the wind." Reclining on his side, Leif brushed the snow from himself and caught his breath.

"I have a candle," said Leif. His breath puffed about him as he rummaged through his rucksack. Remembering his sling pouch, he took out the little food bag. "Ah!"

"What is it?" asked Anna.

"Would you care for a piece of hardtack?" asked Leif.

"Oh, yes—if you can spare it."

"Of course." Leif reached over to Anna. "Here you go. It's hard as stone." She took the piece of hardtack, and he felt the brush of her fingers. He carefully sat up between the branches and reached in the bag for another piece for himself. "I'm famished," said Leif.

"Me, too. It's good," said Anna, sucking on the unleavened biscuit.

"Here's a bit of jerky," said Leif, eating a strip as he held one out to Anna. "It's good and salty. If you weren't thirsty before, this will do the trick."

"*Tack.*" Appetite took them over, and sounds of gnawing,

chewing, sucking, and the tearing of jerky united them in the dark.

"Here's an apple only partly frozen," said Leif.

"Good. *Tack*."

After a moment she said, "I don't know what I would have done if you hadn't come along. Four more miles—I was already getting stiff with cold. Maybe I would have snuck back to the barn."

"Good thing you didn't have to do that. It's a very cold night. . . . I hope you don't mind if I stay under this tree with you," said Leif. In ordinary circumstances, camping out with an unchaperoned young woman was unthinkable. But going out in the dark in such a blizzard to dig another shelter was equally unthinkable. "As the Lord is my witness, I won't harm you."

"Of course. I'm not worried," Anna reassured him. "I'm convinced you are a gentleman, Leif." Leif was relieved. How scandalized the elders would be to know of such a thing as this.

"I don't have much else to eat," said Leif.

"I have nothing," said Anna.

"Will your parents return tomorrow?" Leif wondered what Anna was going to do.

"I—I pray to heaven they will," she said.

What about her uncle Henrik, Leif wondered. But he didn't want to pry, so he was silent. No telling what the brute may have done. Perhaps she was embarrassed.

"And if I may ask," said Anna, "what brought you out here in such weather?" Her voice was musical, but it carried a burden.

"We are out of flour, and our mill is broken. We're stretching our coffee with roasted barley. The store in town hasn't gotten supplies for almost two months." Leif fished his sweater out of the rucksack. "And Ma is ailing and needs medicine." He straightened his buffalo robe beneath him. The light had faded away, and he could no longer see much but shadows—and a hint of a glow here and there above them. He carefully got out of his coat, put on the heavy knitted wool sweater, and put his coat back on.

"I'm sorry about your mother."

"Ya, *tack*. Tomorrow perhaps we can go see if your parents have returned." Leif heard nothing further from Anna, so he lay down on the frozen ground, wrapping his robe around himself. He'd gotten his blood going with the digging. He pulled the earflaps of his raccoon cap down and tied the leather thongs under his chin. Soon he got up again.

Leif pulled out his candle and rustled in the bag for his bundle of Swedish matches. In the dark he bumped his head into a branch and felt around to map out in his mind where the branches were.

"What are you doing?" Anna asked.

"I'm going to light a candle," Leif said. Though he had only a small bundle of Swedish safety matches, this was surely an occasion for some light. He pulled out a match, gripped it in his teeth, and groped in the bag for the striking strip. He struck the match and lighted the candle. He loved the sulfurous smell of burnt matches.

The small tree haven was now bathed in soft light. Anna lay wrapped tightly in the blanket, resting her head on her folded left arm. Strands of blond hair crossed her forehead. Even in the candlelight Leif could see her bright blue eyes. He felt the heat rise in his face once more. A girl made him very anxious. But she acted like a comrade, and that made him easy. He would simply think of her as a friend. His sister, Ellen, came to mind, though she was six years older than he.

"Is it okay?" he asked, wondering if the light invaded her

privacy. He wanted to sit up again, but the only space for that was rather near Anna, where either of them could easily reach over and touch the other. He felt that he needed permission.

"Ya, it's good."

Leif studied Anna. "You don't look so warm yet," he said. He was warm himself for the time being. He'd been walking all day, and then he had tunneled under the tree. And he had the buffalo robe.

"I'll be all right," Anna said. "I feel warmer already."

"I'm such an idiot," Leif said, regretting again that he talked to himself like Pa.

"What?" said Anna.

"Look, here is a sheet of canvas that covered the load on the toboggan. You can wrap up in that, too."

"Are you sure? You already gave me your blanket."

"I have my buffalo robe, a thick sweater, and a good wool coat. You take it." Of course, he was also wearing a woolen union suit. Leif placed the candle near the trunk of the tree and spread the canvas over Anna.

Anna arranged the canvas and the blanket, moving deftly in the tight space. He looked again at her face. Anna drew the blanket and the canvas tightly around herself. She looked at Leif, and Leif smiled a little.

"Is that better?" asked Leif.

"Ya, it's much better," said Anna. The smile that was hidden in the blanket came out in her voice and her eyes.

Suddenly a small avalanche of snow fell upon Anna. "Ah!" she cried. Leif leaped to join her in brushing the snow off, but the physical contact with her body struck him as improper and he drew back. Anna laughed and shook the rest of the snow off. Leif was flustered and retreated.

"It's okay," she said.

"I'm going to light the candle once more," he said. "I have an idea." Leif lit the candle and unwrapped the knife from its rag. He began cutting small sprigs from wherever he could reach them. The lower branches extended into the snowbank around the tree, and Leif had to dig the snow away with his hands to reach most of the supple twigs.

"What are you going to do with those?" Anna asked.

"I'm going to make us each a pillow," Leif answered. Soon he had a pile of limber sprigs. He gathered a bundle of them in his hands and tied it together with the rag that the knife had been wrapped in. "There you go, Anna. A spruce twig pillow."

"Oh, it's the Royal Stockholm Hotel, Leif. Very nice." Leif laughed and cut more sprigs and thought about what he would use to tie the bundle with. He reached for the rifle, slipped the canvas case off of it, and wrapped the case around his bundle.

"There, now. I'm set, too," he said. He blew the candle out again and lay back down. What a strange turn of events.

CHAPTER 3

What Must Be Done

"Anna?" croaked Leif.

"Ya?" came a sleepy reply.

"If the storm keeps your parents from coming home, it will keep your uncle Henrik from leaving, too, won't it?"

"Yes, that's true," she said. She sat up. "And he might be very angry with me. I had barricaded myself in the bedroom. Henrik insisted I come out. He was trying the door and threatening to break in—all the while making a joke of it— so I propped a chair under the doorknob. I dressed the best I could with clothes from the trunk and climbed out the window. I dropped into the drift and ran for the barn. It was slow going, like a nightmare."

Leif whistled. "You must have been terrified."

"Ya," she whispered. "In the barn I watched through the cracks, and I saw Henrik coming. I took the old skis, went out the back, and flew toward the lake without ski poles. Thank goodness it is not far, and it was easier going then. I crossed the lake, and not long after, you found me."

"What were you going to do?" Leif asked.

"The Westrich farm is west of here about four miles. I thought I would try to make it there. I was just so frightened of Henrik. He's a big fellow and crazy as a three-legged goose."

"It would have been a miracle to get that far, I think," said Leif.

"The good Lord was watching over me today," said Anna.

"So then . . . did Henrik . . . did he . . ." Leif began, searching for words.

In silhouette Anna turn her head aside. She was quiet for a moment.

"Oh, he grabbed at me when I was at the stove. I spun around and smacked him hard with a heavy pot, and he fell right on his back. That's when I ran upstairs into the bedroom. Too bad the pot wasn't full of boiling water!"

Leif swallowed. "You're lucky you got away," he said.

"I shouldn't have said that—about the boiling water. I suppose he can't help himself. He is not right in the head. He has spells. Pa told him never to come around—his own brother, mind you."

"Did he know your parents were gone?" Leif asked.

"I have no idea. He is not stupid. He visits farms around the countryside, we've heard, asking to work for a meal and sleeping in barns and sheds. He looks like a tramp and reeks like a billy goat. I feel sorry for him but only at a distance." Leif could hear Anna shudder. He shook his head.

"I sure am thirsty," he said.

"Ya, so am I," said Anna.

"I thought at night I would build a campfire and melt snow in a kettle," said Leif, "but I didn't think of what to do for water in a blizzard. My canteen is empty."

"Guess we'll just have to eat a little snow," said Anna. By the rustling Leif could tell that she had scooped some snow from the bank behind her and eaten it. "That's pretty cold for barely a swallow," she said. "We'll still die of thirst but with frozen tongues."

"I'm going to build a fire to heat the little pot over so we can melt some water," said Leif. "My mouth is dry as a glove."

"You don't think it will melt the snow above and make it fall on us?" asked Anna.

"I mean a very small fire," said Leif. "One that we can put out with a handful of snow." In the darkness Leif retrieved his knife from the base of the spruce's trunk. "I'm going to light the fat lamp, or I'll use up all the matches." Leif lit a candle and fetched the fat lamp and the block of lard from the base of the tree. The lamp was nothing more than a shallow oval bowl made of baked clay.

Leif carved shavings from the lard block into the bowl and draped a length of linen yarn across it, allowing one end to rest in the groove at the bowl's edge. Then he held the bowl over the candle until the lard melted enough to soak the yarn wick. He lit the wick with the candle, blew the candle out, and rested the lamp upon the overturned pewter mug near the base of the tree.

The wick burned along its length to the point where it submerged in the melted fat, and there the yellow flame stood dancing. Once again Anna's face appeared. Leif set about breaking off dry dead sticks from the interior of the tree. Anna joined him, and shortly they had enough to feed a small fire.

"Now our sitting room has a fireplace," said Leif. He made a bed of the larger sticks and then built a small nest upon it from the others. He lighted a twig in the flame of the fat lamp and used it to light the nest. He nursed the fire while he held the snow-packed pot over it.

"Good," said Anna. "You hold the pot, and I will handle the fire." They sat cross-legged on opposite sides of the tiny fire, embraced by the bows of the spruce.

"What church is the new preacher that your parents went to meet?"

"Covenant," said Anna.

"My parents go to the Baptist meeting when the preacher comes around," Leif said. "Though Pa doesn't care much for church. He'd rather sit on a log in the woods."

"It depends on the minister," said Anna. "If he preaches hellfire and damnation and doesn't allow dancing, I won't go either," she said.

"Amen to that," said Leif. "Look, it's starting to melt." Tendrils of steam were rising from the snow in the pot. "Anna, would you grab a handful of snow and add it to the pot?"

"Sure." Anna reached back and scooped up a lump of snow and added it to the steaming pot. Then she broke off a few more twigs and added them to the fire. She had taken the canvas food sack and tied it on her head like a bonnet, and her blue eyes shone in the flickering light. Leif liked her expressions and her quick smile.

"Try it," Leif said. "Take a sip."

"All right." She took the pot, touching his fingers again. "It's icy cold but liquid." They added snow from time to time until the pot was half full of water. They continued heating it until it was warm.

"Have a drink, Leif." Leif drank several gulps, moaned with pleasure, and handed the pot back to Anna. Anna drank.

"Go ahead and finish it," Leif said.

"No, you have another drink." Leif took another drink and gave the pot to Anna.

"Finish it," he said. Leif pushed the fire apart with a stick. Embers glowed orange as the wan light of the fat lamp took over again.

With the fire out and the snow-melting job done, the cold returned. Leif and Anna drew their coverings about themselves and sat in silence as the embers between them faded into small points.

"I can't keep my eyes open any longer," he said with a yawn. "Good night, Anna."

"Good night, Leif."

CHAPTER 4

God Will Forgive Us

Leif woke several times cold, stretched and tensed himself to warm up, and drifted off again. Finally he came fully awake. He could not get warm. Cold from the ground soaked through even the buffalo robe. He turned toward Anna and listened. She seemed restless, too. Perhaps she was as cold as he.

"Anna," Leif whispered in the darkness.

"Ya," said Anna.

"Are you cold?"

"Ya. I can't sleep," she said, her voice clipped.

"We must bundle together to stay warm, then," Leif said, shivering.

"I used to sleep between my brothers on cold nights."

"So did I." Leif quickly moved next to Anna. "Let's spread the hides out and put the horse blanket down and wrap up together in the buffalo robe and tarp. And I want you to put on my sweater."

"Are you sure? You are cold, too." Leif was already taking off his overcoat, lying back to stay clear of the low-hanging branches.

"Anna, I have a woolen union suit, a vest, a wool overcoat, and a warm cap. Please take the sweater." He held it out to her.

"All right. Thank you." Anna briskly removed her sack bonnet and wriggled out of her hooded woolen jersey. She put on the sweater and got back into her bonnet and jersey. "There now. I'm all set."

They folded the woolen horse blanket and laid it upon the animal hides. Anna lay down on her left side with her back to Leif, and they drew the buffalo robe and canvas over themselves. Leif did not dare to put his arm around her, so he folded it against his chest. They huddled together, and the combined heat of their bodies warmed them both.

"Ah, it's much better, isn't it?" said Leif, enormously grateful for the warmth and comfort. Lying on the hides and blanket made a difference for him, too.

"Ya, it's good, much better," said Anna, breathing deeply. Leif felt her shivering subside.

"God will forgive us," Leif said.

"Of course. I believe that," said Anna, "but we have done nothing wrong to forgive."

"Do you think so?" Leif asked. "The old ones would have a fit if they knew."

"Perhaps. But they would know only the gossip, not the truth, and maybe they will never know."

"Hm," murmured Leif. "I hope you are right." They drifted into sleep while the great storm wrapped them more deeply in snow and carried away the last breaths of heat from the land. Leif's dreams were fitful.

"I will be back for chores by morning," said Rollie.
"No! I said no, and I mean NO!" thundered Pa.

"It's to be the biggest barn dance of the year. Håkan Skratthult will be there with his band."

Pa slammed his hand down on the table. "I don't want to hear another word about it."

Rollie bolted up and went for the door.
Pa barked, "Where do you think you're going?"

"Leif, Leif." Anna pushed him gently. Leif's mind swam upward to dim gray light. His heart leaped and began to pound. He was snuggled with a girl. He could see their breath rising. "You were wrestling with a ghost," said Anna.

"Sorry."

"It's okay."

Leif tried to recall what he'd been dreaming. "I think it must be dawn; there's light. I'm going to go up and see."

"All right," Anna said.

They lay still for a while. Leif's mind was spinning.

"All right," Leif said. He slid from beneath the robe and tarp and tucked them around Anna. He put on his iron-stiff boots and crawled over to fetch the shovel. He tried to move the toboggan from the trench opening but could not budge it. "It's buried in snow," he said. "I'll dig a new trench beside it."

Leif crawled under the branches beyond where he had been lying earlier and began scooping snow away, tunneling out from the tree. He carved snow away, one shovel after another, and still did not break through to the surface. He paused to rest a moment. Suddenly he dropped the shovel and scooted back to Anna and lay down beside her.

"Hello, friend."

"Hello. My turn!" said Anna, and she abandoned the covers for the shovel. She burrowed with great energy, and Leif lay smiling, listening to her muttering and scraping.

"Leif, I think we are buried until spring."

"That's too bad," he said cheerily, leaning on his elbow and gazing at Anna's shadowy form as she bustled back and forth in the dim light with scoops of snow.

"Your turn again," she said at last, crawling back to where Leif lay.

"Mustn't lie around all day," said Leif. He crept back to the tunnel and resumed digging. "The light is brighter at the top," he said. "It's more than six feet now. I'm going to put the snowshoes on."

Leif at last poked through. "Aha!" he cried. He looked up through the ragged hole in the top of the tunnel and saw stars. White light played on the edges of the hole. He lifted his snowshoes free of the snow that had fallen on them and carved more snow away until he was able to emerge from the tunnel. A bright moon was shining, and a very cold wind was blowing.

Leif descended back into the cavity beneath the tree. "Anna," he said, catching his breath, "there must be eight feet of snow drifted around the tree."

"Lord in heaven, I've never seen such a thing." Anna cried. "Let me look."

"Put the snowshoes on," said Leif. He untied the snowshoes from his boots and in the dim light helped Anna strap them on. She climbed up the passageway and all was silent. Anna came back down and crouched in the deep shadow of the cavity.

"Leif, I've never seen such snow. It's very cold but so beautiful."

"I thought it must be dawn, but it's the moon," said Leif. Anna untied the snowshoes and crawled to where Leif lay. "I'm going to go up and look around," said Leif. He tied the snowshoes on and climbed up to the surface. The wind was strong, and he could not see very far through the blowing snow, but the moon was shining bright. He might be able to travel himself, but Anna wasn't dressed well enough. He climbed back down.

"It's too cold and windy to go anywhere now," he said as he began shoveling snow back into the opening. "I'm going to plug the hole so it won't get so cold in here."

"Ya, I can feel the cold air coming down," said Anna.

"Let's eat something," Leif said.

"That would suit me," said Anna. Leif groped in the dim light and found the apples and hardtack and jerky, and they ate.

"When we leave, I will have to dig out the toboggan," said Leif. "First we must go to your house and see if Henrik is still there. And I must go on to Freeport. But what if Henrik is still there? Then you must come with me. If Henrik is gone, can you give me some food?"

"Of course, Leif. What a mess I've made for you."

"You did nothing wrong. We have made friends. That's good, isn't it?"

She smiled at him and nodded. "Ya, it is. But how will we get food if Henrik is still there?"

"I have the rifle, but hunting will be no good now. All the game will be snowed in; nothing will be moving but owls and crows, maybe a few hares. We could go back home to my parents' house, but they're already short of food. Still, they have some. Or we could go to your neighbors' house to the west."

"There must be a way to deal with Henrik," said Anna. "Maybe I could go to the house while you wait and see what state he's in."

"I don't see how he could have left. He has to be there," said Leif. "What if he is wild? What then? If he is such a big lout, I won't be able to stop him if he comes after us, but I don't want to hurt him."

"No, you can't hold him. But if you are there, he might not bother me. He's not completely wild; he just gets ideas and gets excited and can't contain himself, especially if he's gotten his hands on some wine. But around strangers he keeps himself more in check. Of course, I can't be sure. . . ."

"Well, it's just two miles, so maybe it's worth going to take a look. If he tries anything, he can't hold us both down at once, and I've seen that you can handle yourself."

Anna smiled and looked down.

"Still, you can't stay there with him," Leif said, "so let's try to get some food and your winter clothes."

"You're right. It might be days before my parents get back. The horses will have slow going pulling the sleigh through all this snow," said Anna. She pursed her lips. "Ah, I've made such a mess for you."

"Anna, no," Leif said. "Do you think I am not grateful that I found you—that you did not wind up with terrible frostbite or worse? We are neighbors, and now we are friends. If you ask me, it's a great piece of luck."

Anna shook her head. "I can't thank you enough for being willing to go back with me to face Henrik."

CHAPTER 5

Anna's House

"What direction across the lake is your farm?" Leif asked.

"East, more or less."

"We will have the wind at our backs, then. I think we might as well go now. We've eaten a little, and it's light enough to see. The wind might blow for days."

Anna took a deep breath. "I agree. Let's go." She took her makeshift bonnet off and handed it to Leif. "Here's the food sack."

"Why don't you keep it on your head, Anna? We can put the food in the rucksack. I'll put it in the bottom and put the pot over it."

Leif packed the rucksack and loaded the toboggan. It was difficult for Anna to climb out of the tunnel without snowshoes, so Leif planted his feet and pulled her up.

Anna pulled her skis from the snowbank where she had stuck them and bent to fix her feet in the bindings. "Ah!" she cried.

"What's wrong?" asked Leif.

"Look! The clip has come off the ski." Leif took a look.

"Ya, we can't fix this out here. It's a job for the shop. But I can pull you on the toboggan." Anna narrowed her eyes and planted her mitts on her hips.

"All right, but I must insist on one thing."

"What would that be?"

"I am no sack of flour. You must allow me to pull you on the toboggan half the way."

"But Anna, you don't . . . "

"I insist. I won't move from here unless you agree."

Leif laughed. "All right, I agree. But in that case I'd like you to wear my buffalo robe while you are pulling."

"All right, then. Let's go." Anna sat down upon the hides facing the front, for the wind still blew strongly out of the west. Leif tied the rucksack down behind her as she settled herself upon the blanket and wrapped up in the tarp.

"Still pretty windy, isn't it?" called Leif as he moved to the front of the toboggan.

"Ya," replied Anna, her voice muffled by the tarp over her face.

"Hold tight," called Leif as he tugged at the lead line and trudged east across the great frozen dunes toward the lake. His buffalo robe flapped about his legs, and the wind picked up the powder broken by his snowshoes and sent it scudding ahead. Progress was slow not just because Anna was on the toboggan but also because they were breaking a trail a foot deep in newly fallen snow.

When they reached the lake, the snow crust formed by the wind became more dense, and Leif was able to make better headway. But immediately he stopped. "I'm too warm. I must take off this robe. You can wear it."

"All right," said Anna with a skeptical frown. She put the hooded robe on and wrapped her legs in the tarp.

Out upon the lake, away from the shorelines, Leif saw that the sky was growing light ahead of them. Anna called to him, "Oh, isn't it beautiful?"

"Ah, yes. It's breathtaking." Leif stopped and looked up. Some stars were visible through the haze of fine snow in the air, and the bright moon had a halo.

"My turn," she sang.

"Not yet," said Leif. He took the line and started off again at a brisk pace.

When they had reached the middle of the lake, Anna called out, "It is time to change places. Come now, you agreed."

"All right, then." Leif sat down on the toboggan and removed the snowshoes. Anna tied them on her feet and stood up.

"Why don't you start out with the buffalo robe? If you get too warm, you can give it to me. But I had a heavier coat underneath, so you may want to keep it."

Leif sat down on the toboggan and wrapped himself in the tarp. The surface of the toboggan was much harder than the earth under the spruce tree, even with the horse blanket beneath him.

Anna started off, and Leif was impressed with her strength and energy. He watched her pulling for a while and saw that his robe made a pleasing shape as the wind wrapped it around her form. As if sensing his thoughts, Anna turned and smiled. Leif grinned sheepishly. Then he slid down and lay back against the rucksack, looking up at the moon and feeling the snow slide underneath.

"Anna," Leif called, sitting up. Anna stopped and came to squat beside Leif.

"What is it?" she asked.

"Could I come and visit you?"

"I would like that."

"But what if it's forbidden?"

"Forbidden by whom?"

"Your father, of course."

Anna pressed her lips tight.

"Oh, don't worry so much. Why would he forbid it?"

"He's religious."

"But he's not unjust. Besides, I'm of age. Don't worry." Leif looked at Anna's serious expression and grinned. She smiled back at him and resumed pulling the toboggan. Leif looked out across the glistening snow. This was not a girl who would be blown about by the wind. He liked that about her. The snow whispered under the toboggan.

The whispering stopped. Anna stood looking intently at the darkness of the trees on the shore. She turned to him. "We're almost there. We're going into the deep snow again. You can take over." Leif stood up and let the canvas tarp and blanket drop onto the toboggan. They exchanged the snowshoes.

"You can keep the robe for now," he said to Anna. The trees along the shoreline acted as a break against the wind, and he felt warm in his wool coat.

"All right."

They both said little, not knowing what they would find, dreading what they might.

"We'll see what we see." Leif pulled the toboggan and walked toward the shore. The sky had grown lighter. He leaned into the rope and pulled the toboggan up onto the snow-mounded land, which rose steeply at first but then flattened out. Dark trees began to enclose them.

"Head a little to the left, where the snow leads off to a point there," said Anna. Leif turned and the snow rasped softly under the toboggan. As he paced on, the snowshoes squeaked in the snow, and Leif tried to step more quietly.

"I see the barn," said Leif.

"Ya, let's go to the back." The wind had swept most of the snow clear of the doors. With a little shoveling, Leif was able to open them.

CHAPTER 6

A Jarring Discovery

Once inside the barn, Anna bustled about as if it were broad daylight. Leif could see next to nothing, but he could smell hay and manure. The horses nickered softly. Anna took his arm and pulled him along, and in six paces he was standing next to the warm, massive body of a horse. He stroked the horse's shaggy coat and spoke to her in a low, soothing voice.

"Hello there, girl. My name is Leif. I'm pleased to meet you. Good girl." As his eyes adjusted to the deep shadows of the barn, he could see the other horses, three cows, and several goats, all huddling close to each other in the straw.

Anna spoke. "The horses are Hansel, Gretel, Jack, and Frida. I must milk the cows right away, clean the stalls, and put down hay for the animals. But the milk pails are in the house." They looked at each other without smiling.

Anna fetched a scoop shovel, and they went back out the rear door. Leif put his snowshoes on and helped Anna onto the toboggan. They advanced around the barn toward the farm-house.

"Look, the snow is almost up to the second-floor window on this side," said Leif. "I don't see any smoke coming from the chimney."

"Maybe we're in luck, ya?" said Anna. Leif pulled the

toboggan slowly toward the house. "Let's dig out my good skis and poles, just in case."

"Good idea," said Leif. They approached the front porch on the south side of the farmhouse. Snow covered the door.

"He is either gone or has run out of firewood and can't get out, I think," said Leif.

"But he could climb out the upstairs window," said Anna.

"So maybe he is gone." Leif began digging where Anna showed him the skis would be. "At least if he is inside, he won't be rushing out to surprise us, ya?" Leif said in a low voice. Shortly Leif discovered the skis and poles, pulled them out of the drift, and handed them to Anna. She laid them across the toboggan, tied the bindings to her feet, and stepped into the snow, holding her scoop shovel.

"I'll help you dig. The front door is here," she said, nodding at the spot. "Pa built a new porch but hasn't put a roof over it yet." They dug until the top half of the door was cleared.

"Henrik!" she called.

"Anna, if he threatens us, I am going to pull you up to the toboggan, and we'll head for the back of the barn. You can put your skis on there, and he won't catch us in this deep snow."

"Henrik!" Anna called again. No answer. Anna knocked on the door with the handle of her shovel. No response came from inside, so they continued digging away the snow. "Henrik!" Anna called one last time as they cleared the porch floor in front of the door.

Leif opened the door a crack and called, "Henrik!" They went in and looked warily around. The house was stone-cold.

"Let me light a lantern, Leif, and we'll go through the whole place." They moved from the kitchen area into the sitting room and opened Anna's parents' bedroom door. No Henrik. They looked beyond the staircase into the back room, which was full of tools, baskets, garden implements, a small flour mill, and other miscellany, and then they went up the stairs.

"This used to be one room," said Anna, "shared by my brothers and me. But when I was ten years old, Pa made a separate room for me. It's pretty small, as you can see," she said, opening the door.

"So you jumped out of a second-floor window!" said Leif.

"The snow was deep," said Anna. "Looks like Henrik is gone." They went back downstairs. Anna loaded the cast iron kitchen stove with wood and lit it. "I want to get those cows milked, and then how about a hot meal and some coffee?"

"That sounds good." Leif picked up two milk pails from a wooden stand near the door. "Are two pails enough?" asked Leif.

"Ya," said Anna. "I don't know where the other pail is. Only Agata and Beata give milk, anyway. Carina quit." Anna put on her winter coat, and they went out on the porch. Leif tied on his snowshoes and fetched Anna's skis from the toboggan. She put them on, scurried up the steep incline of snow, and was halfway to the barn before Leif had gone ten paces. "Come on, slowpoke," she called, laughing. Leif grinned and trotted after her.

Since the front barn doors were drifted shut, they went around to the rear doors again. Anna had already stepped out of her skis and gone into the darkness. The sun had risen behind the clouds, but the early light revealed an eerie snowscape in which buildings and trees seemed half drowned in white swells. It had been a mighty storm. Leif stood inside the door waiting for his eyes to adjust to the darkness.

In the middle of the barn Anna lit a lantern and walked over to the cows. Suddenly she screamed. "Leif!"

Leif hurried toward her.

"What is it, Anna?"

"Leif! Oh, God! Leif, it's Henrik!" A hairy, bearded man lay slumped against a post. The hairs on Leif's neck stood on end, and his heart jumped to his throat. He took the lantern from Anna and knelt on one knee beside Henrik. He put his hand inside the coat on the man's chest.

"His heart is beating," said Leif.

"Oh, my God," said Anna. "Look how his leg is turned!"

"Do you think it's broken?" asked Leif.

"Beata is touchy," said Anna. "She will kick if you don't move just right. Henrik must have been trying to milk her. Look, there's the pail."

"We must get him in the house." Leif quickly brought the toboggan.

"We can put down straw on the dirt and pull him to the doors," said Anna.

"Let's put the horse blanket down to lay him on, so we can get him off the toboggan easier," said Leif.

Together they managed to get Henrik into the house. Gripping the ends of the blanket, they moved him to a pallet on the floor near the stove. He was simply too heavy to put anywhere else.

"What should we do?" wondered Leif aloud.

"I don't know," said Anna. "I'll put some warm towels on his face. He was in the freezing barn, so he will warm up in here."

"He needs a doctor."

"Ya. I'll ski to the neighbors and try to get someone to go for a doctor. I'll melt a kettle of snow and get the pump thawed. Would you put straw down for the animals? And I'll get water ready for them."

"Ya, that's good. Of course." Leif immediately left for the

barn. He was anxious to be on his way to Freeport, but this was a real emergency. Anna needed to settle the animals so she could leave to get a doctor for Henrik. There would be no coffee and porridge, but that was a small thing now.

When Leif returned to the house, he clasped Anna's hands. Words poured out of him. "Anna, I want more than anything to stay with you now, and I would stay with Henrik while you go, but I must get on to Freeport. I feel so torn. I will come back as soon as I can.

"Ya, I know you must go. All we can do is pray. Godspeed! Come when you can."

"Anna? Suppose your parents come home today and your pa is able to go for a doctor. If you can, would you check on my parents? They won't know I've been delayed, and I don't know how the storm has left them. Only go if you have a chance and aren't needed here."

"Of course. If I can, I will."

Leif paced rapidly westward across the lake. He followed the tracks that he and Anna had laid coming in. Anna had stuffed his food sack with Swedish sausage, hardtack, and sweet apple slices. The sausage and apple slices would freeze, but they could still be chewed. The sausage had been smoked and could be shaved with a sharp knife. He worried about his ma, but he was doing the best he could. He walked in the snowshoes as if in a dream.

CHAPTER 7
Fischer's Tavern

In the advancing darkness Leif trudged down the deeply drifted main street of Freeport toward the only building with a lighted window. "Fischer's Tavern" read a sign that swung gently on its chains above the boardwalk. A few horses and sleighs stood around the building. With his scoop shovel Leif carved a flat shelf in the snowdrift that lay against the front of the tavern. He set his snowshoes and the shovel into the snow on the shelf and hefted his toboggan up on top of them. A man came out the door, opening a shaft of smoky light and spilling out a dull roar of voices and the music of an accordion. The door closed behind the man, and he lurched off into the blue dusk.

Carrying his rucksack and rifle, Leif opened the door and walked inside. Loud chatter, laughter, music, and the clatter of boots upon the plank floor filled his ears. The air was thick with the haze and smells of pipe tobacco and woodsmoke and the aromas of whisky, beer, venison stew, and men who hadn't bathed in a month or two. Above the bar in front of him was a sign that read "Overnight accommodations, 35 cents." Another sign gave tribute to three local men who had died at Gettysburg in the War of the Rebellion. Leif walked to the back of the room and propped his gear in a corner.

He beheld the raucous crowd for only a moment before he

moved to the large main stove, a grand nickel-plate affair whose cast iron sides glowed raspberry red. He shucked his mitts and lifted the raccoon cap off his head. Jamming them into the pockets of his buffalo robe, Leif held his hands to the glowing stove and looked around without meeting anyone's eyes. A barkeep nearby gave him a friendly nod. He nodded shyly back and relaxed a little. No one challenged him. He was just one of the crowd.

"Say, young fella, ye wouldn't have any tobacco on ye, would ye?" asked a scarlet-cheeked man with a fouled beard and glazed eyes.

"No, sir. Sorry," said Leif with a tight smile. People clustered around the three stoves or blew steam at each other at the bar. Kerosene lamps burned here and there. Fully stoked, the three woodstoves could hardly keep the drafty place warm enough to allow patrons to take off their heavy coats, and few had.

A man wearing a blue wool Union army coat came up to Leif and offered him a tureen of house stew. "Here, you might could use some o' this, eh, young man? Fella ordered it, but he fell off his stool before he took a bite. Out like a light," he chuckled.

"What? Well—thanks." Leif took the bowl and a large biscuit from the man. He found a seat on a bench against the wall and lifted the bowl to his mouth. The stew was good and thick and still warm, steaming around his head. It smelled of venison, and Leif discovered bear meat in it and potatoes, onions, carrots, parsnips, and some kind of squash. Winter fare. As he ate, he noticed two women talking in the far corner. A small child lay asleep upon the table, and one of the women held an infant.

Leif ate the stew and the biscuit, set the tureen under the bench, and pulled a stool up to the stove. With a hot meal in his belly, he took off his buffalo coat and boots, unbuttoned his wool jacket, and set his mind on thawing his feet and drying his wool socks. He wondered where he might stay the night. Maybe the tavern had a stable where he could bed down on a pile of straw.

Fragments of a dozen conversations reached Leif.

"Three days they were stuck," one man said to another as they bent over a checkerboard near a stove. "Drift covered the tracks fourteen feet deep." The tall man's Adam's apple bobbed under his beard.

"And that's what I told him," a rattling, nasal voice said. "You're too late, friend. I filed my claim six months ago."

"And Ole says, 'So, what's time to a pig?'" Laughter erupted.

". . . the post office and thirty acres . . ."

". . . ah, quit yer bellyachin'."

"That's about the size of it. . . ."

"I couldn't believe my eyes."

"You sure can't be sitting on the fence, mister."

The unaccustomed heat amid the laughter and the roil of voices suddenly struck Leif with a great drowsiness, and his head dropped to his chest. He lifted it up, but soon it dropped again. He returned to the bench against the wall and sat himself down.

Someone gently shook his shoulder, and he looked into the alert brown eyes of the bartender he'd seen earlier.

"Time to go, lad," the man said. Leif sat up and looked about, gripping the edge of the bench. Three or four men remained talking, and most of the lamps had been put out. Leif stood up. He walked over to the barkeep, who was removing ashes from the nickel-plate stove.

"'Scuse me, sir. I just walked into town. 'Spose I could sleep in the stable tonight?"

The barkeep ducked his head down low and spoke quietly to Leif. "You can sleep on the bench behind the back stove there," he said. "It's a cold one tonight." Leif looked at the bench. It was narrow, but it would get him off the floor. And he'd be inside, next to a stove.

"*Tack*—thank you kindly," said Leif.

"You're welcome. I'm Klaus Fischer. What's your name, son?"

"Leif Eliasson," said Leif as they shook hands.

"Bjorn's boy?"

"Yes, sir." Mr. Fischer smiled and nodded.

"There's a stack of green birch out the back door there. If you stoke the stove with that, it'll burn all night."

"Thank you, sir." Mr. Fischer started to walk away, then turned back.

"Mr. Eliasson, I assume you know how to trim lamp wicks?"

"Yes, sir."

"How about in the morning you go around and trim the lamps, take the ashes out, stoke the stoves, and fill the woodbox, and I'll pay you a dime and feed you breakfast to boot."

"Sure, Mr. Fischer."

Leif stoked the stove, and after trying the narrow bench, he decided to sleep on the floor. Couldn't fall as far from there.

Leif hardly remembered lying down to sleep, but when he woke on the floor curled up in his buffalo robe and raccoon cap, it was still pitch-black. A dull red glow under the stove showed the fire was still alive. Anna leaped to mind. He wondered if her parents had returned or if she had gotten a doctor to look after Henrik. With a broken leg, Henrik certainly would not be a threat to her for a long time. He might even have frozen his feet and hands. Leif could hardly wait to return home. He would visit Anna as soon as possible.

He rose up on his elbow. Ah yes, he was to trim the wicks and stoke the stoves. Someone was stirring about in the kitchen behind the L-shaped bar, and a kerosene lamp flickered. Leif walked around the bar and entered the kitchen.

"Hello?" he called.

"Go to hell! It's too early yet!" A wiry old man appeared and scowled at Leif. "Be another half hour yet afore coffee," he said.

"Okay," said Leif. "I'm s'posed to trim the lamp wicks." The man disappeared and returned.

"A' right, here's a pair o' shears. Take that lamp from the post there so ye can see what yer doin.' And I want these back when yer done."

"Okay," said Leif, taking the shears. He lifted the lamp off the post and went about trimming the wicks. "Should I light them, then, as I go?" he called.

"Hell, I don't care a flyin' fiddle what ye do," said the old geezer. The man carried a kettle of water out to the nickel-plate stove and set it on top, then jammed some more firewood into it and clanged the door shut.

Leif trimmed the wicks of half a dozen lamps and lit two of them so that folks could make their way about. He took the shears back to the kitchen and stood at the door. The cook took the shears. "Go fetch me that kettle o' water now, boy."

"Yes, sir," said Leif. He brought the kettle back, and the cook hefted it onto the cast iron range. Leif gave him a nod and left to clean the ashes out of the woodstoves. He filled them with firewood and tinder sticks, but two had gone cold and needed lighting. Rather than ask for matches and risk the ire of the grumpy cook, Leif shoveled some burning coals from the nickel-plate stove. His fingers turned gold in the red light that breathed out when he opened the door of the stove.

As he began filling the woodbox, he heard people clunking down the stairs and scraping stools up to the bar.

"Just hold yer horses. The coffee'll be up in a few minutes," yelled the cook from the kitchen. Leif sat down at one of the plank tables and yawned. Soon the cook brought a large kettle of coffee around and filled everyone's mugs. When he got to Leif, he cocked an eyebrow and said, "Say, young fella, ya wanna earn some money? My helper didn't come in this morning."

"Yes, sir, I would be willing to help you, but I can't stay long, 'cause my mother is ailing, and I need to . . ."

"Oh, don't worry, boy. It won't take long. Just help me get these people fed. I'll pay ye twenty-five cents."

"Well, all right, but just for breakfast; then I'll be on my way. What do you need done, Mr. Cook?" Leif got up from the bench.

"Pass those forks and pewter plates around to folks that have tokens, and then get ready for the platters I'm fixin' to load up. Put them pitchers of maple syrup out and the butter. Then take the coffee kettle around again." By now most of the folks who'd been making so much noise last night had come down and taken seats. There were a few more women and older kids he hadn't seen before.

Mr. Fischer appeared at the counter and was taking money from people who were paying their overnight and breakfast charges. The place wasn't as bawdy as last night. Children and ladies were present; it had more of a family feel to it. Mr. Fischer refused to serve beer and liquor before noon.

Soon Leif was hustling about serving coffee and pancakes, filling syrup pitchers, and collecting dirty dishes. People were eating, talking, and heaving bags about. The door opened and revealed the blue world that came just before dawn.

Finally Leif stacked a plate with pancakes, poured himself

a mug of coffee, and sat down to eat. When someone banged his empty syrup pitcher on the bar, he got up and filled it, then resumed eating. The cook strutted out to take a look at the situation, spotted Leif, and yelled, "Sittin' down on the job, eh? Yer fired!"

"I say, 'You're hired!'" countered Mr. Fischer, scowling at the cook. "You want a job, Mr. Eliasson? I'll put you to work right now. Fifty cents a day, room and board."

"Sir? Excuse me, Sir? What time does the train stop in this town?" The tall man with the Adam's apple addressed Mr. Fischer.

"Nine thirty-five, sir. Might be running late today." Mr. Fischer turned to answer other questioners who were anxious to make sure they wouldn't miss their connections.

"Stagecoach to Holdingford is here! Loading up!" a man called from the door.

"That ain't no coach! That's a sleigh! And look at the size of those horses!" someone yelled.

"Them are Belgians!" called another.

"Antonio, quick, run uppa de stair an' get Mama!" instructed a man with a huge black mustache holding two small children on his lap. A boy of about ten sprinted up the stairs screaming, "Mama! Mama!"

"What do you say, Mr. Eliasson?" The interruptions had given Leif a chance to think. It had never occurred to him that he could do something with his life other than stay on the farm with his pa or fling himself into the wild world like his brothers had. He loved books and reading, but his family had no means to send him to teacher's college.

"Mr. Fischer, I'm much obliged, and I'd like to do it, but I got to get back. My ma needs medicine, and we need supplies at the house. I got to get back soon as I can." He was already running late and, besides, he wanted to get home. And visit Anna.

Mr. Fischer nodded. "I see." He thought for a moment. "I can use a good man like you, Leif. Stop by next time you're in town, and let's see if we can work something out."

"Thank you, Mr. Fischer. I will," said Leif. "Ah, Mr. Fischer?"

"Yes?"

"How do I find a lady named Mrs. Charbonnier? Ma calls her the root lady. "

"She lives out in the woods a few miles west of town. Talk to Mrs. Reimers at Pulaski's General Store. They're just down the street."

They shook hands. "Ah, Mr. Fischer," Leif said, feeling the color rise in his face. "Excuse me, sir, but the cook said he'd pay me twenty-five cents for helping with breakfast."

"Of course. And I owe you a dime for trimming the lamps and feeding the stoves. You did a good job." He opened the register and paid Leif thirty-five cents. Leif liked Mr. Fischer, all right. He was a straight shooter. And Leif didn't often hear someone say to him, "You did a good job."

Leif walked down to the general store. When he opened the door into Pulaski's, his eyes bugged out at the apples, crackers, honey, pickled herring, pickled cucumbers, prunes, cheese, shoes and shoe leather, vinegar, smoked ham, cloth, coffee, molasses, fresh-cut plug tobacco, and jars of candy. Here he would find a gift for Anna.

Behind the counter a tall, thin woman climbed a stepladder to fetch a red woolen union suit for a customer. On shelves around the store were folded blankets, spools of thread, wooden pails, lanterns, and bottles and cans with curious labels. On the floor in front of the counter stood butter churns, bags of beans, and wooden barrels. "Can I help you, young man?"

He looked up from a large glass candy jar. "Yes, please. Would you give me a scoop of this red-stripe hard rock candy?" He took a breath. "And a bag of licorice."

"That'll be six cents." He laid down his copper pennies.

Kind of a steep price, but he didn't often have a chance to get store-boughten treats. "Ma'am, can you tell me how to get to the root lady's place?"

Mrs. Reimers gave Leif directions. Leif collected his gear and the toboggan and walked out of town to the west, keeping an eye peeled for a split white oak where the trail branched off.

What people would do if the snow continued to pile up, he couldn't imagine. No longer was the world made up of the land and the sky; it was now the land, the snow, and the sky. People had become moles. They seemed to spend half their time digging.

Already it was everywhere eight and ten feet deep and sometimes up to second-floor windows. One man at the tavern had dug a tunnel from house to barn that was completely covered. Teams of horses had a mighty struggle until the snow was packed down or removed. Clydesdales, Belgians, timber sledges, and many men and women shoveling were required to clear a passage through the main street in town.

Leif had seen his first dog team and sled. Now that was the trick. Dogs were light enough that they could run on top of the drifts instead of sinking like horses. He'd heard talk at the tavern that dog teams were carrying the mail in some places. The local postmaster's son had come back from Duluth with a dog team and driver.

CHAPTER 8

Mrs. Charbonnier

Leif stopped a hundred yards from the cabin while the ugliest dog he had ever seen barked his guts out. The creature's dark brown fur was so thick and matted that he looked like a misshapen bear or a giant badger. Snow and ice and bits of sticks and dried leaves were stuck to him. His bark was so savage, it felt like the sheer hatred in him would peel the skin off your face if you looked at him.

Leif was duly terrified. He had begun backing off when suddenly the barking stopped and the dog bowed, pawed the air, and rolled over in submission. A tiny old woman had come out of the woods on snowshoes and approached the dog. "Napoleon, Napoleon, *mon cher*, hoosh! hoosh! *C'est un ami!*" She turned to Leif. "Come on, son. He's a pussycat. He got no teeth."

She couldn't be much over four-and-a-half-feet tall. Her own toothless brown face was wizened to flannel. "I am so glad you came today," she said. "So much snow. I can barely climb out my door." Indeed, her little cabin was very nearly engulfed in a great drift. "Come in. Let's have a little coffee, *oui?*"

"I'd be pleased to do that, Mrs. Charbonnier. But first let me shovel the snow from your door so you can come and go." Leif noticed that the cabin's chimney barely cleared the snow on the roof. He'd take care of that next.

"My name is Leif Eliasson," he said.

"And I am Eartha Charbonnier. You come on inside then, and we'll have some hot coffee." Lively as a river gnome, she descended into the steep hole at her door and went inside. Fortunately the door opened inwards.

"All right, be right there." Leif set to digging more snow out of the pit Mrs. Charbonnier had managed to make in front of her door. All he could do was dig a longer path down from the top, so it wasn't so steep for the old woman.

"Just hang your things on a peg there," said Mrs. Charbonnier, waving at the wall beside the door, "and sit down here by the stove." Having left his buffalo robe on the toboggan outside, Leif hung his snowshoes and wool jacket on pegs and sat down. It was stifling hot in the small cabin, so soon he took off his fur-lined vest as well. Mrs. Charbonnier handed him a mug of black coffee. Her hands were gnarled as ginger roots.

"Thank you, ma'am."

"All the snow keeps it pretty toasty in here, *n'est-ce pas?* For an old one like me, that's a good thing," she chuckled. True, the snow kept the cabin snug. Leif grinned and nodded at her as he sipped the strong hot brew. When Mrs. Charbonnier smiled, he could see she wasn't entirely toothless.

Leif described his ma's symptoms to Mrs. Charbonnier. "She has pains under here," he said, showing her the way Ma had instructed, "and it's worst when Pa is ranting or having a temper and won't talk." He answered her questions as best he could. "And Ma told me to give you this." He handed her the black velvet pouch.

Sitting in her wooden armchair, the old woman opened the pouch and looked inside, puckered her lips slightly, and drew the pouch closed again. She held the pouch in her lap and sat silent for a long time. No sound but faint crackles and sighs from the fire broke the profound stillness of that snow-muffled cabin.

Leif came to with a start. He must have dozed off. It seemed only a moment had passed. Mrs. Charbonnier still looked into space, but the light had shifted. Presently she turned her gaze to him. "You can take this," she said, handing the pouch back to him. "I will give you something to take to your mama. Now listen carefully, *mon cher*. I think your mama might have gall-stones. They can cause a lot of pain, but sometimes the remedy takes care of them.

"Tell her to drink nothing but apple cider vinegar for four days straight: one-half cup at a time, five times a day. And on the second, third, and fourth days, drink a quarter of a cup of apple cider vinegar and a quarter of a cup of nut or seed oil mixed together. She might need to do this over again two or three times, but wait a couple weeks in between. The stones might pass. If gallstones not the problem, the remedy will not hurt her."

Mrs. Charbonnier rose from her rocker. "Now say it back to me so I know you got it." As he did so, she laid some dried plants on the table and chopped the roots into small pieces. She wrapped them in a piece of cloth. "Take this back to your mama. Tell her to make a tea whenever she feel worried and has no peace inside." She turned back to the table and rubbed some plants between her hands so that the leaves were crushed. She wrapped the mass in a square of cloth and handed it to Leif.

"This is a tea for your papa." Leif was surprised that Pa would need a tea. "*M'sieur* Leif, I will speak plain truth to you. Sometimes Papa has trouble. He has worry, or something make him angry, all the time angry. . . ."

"Yes, that's for true. That's how it is with Pa."

"Papa hard to live with. And Mama feel worried and nervous."

"Ya, and so do I—and very sad." Mrs. Charbonnier pursed her lips, closed her eyes, and nodded.

"You see, *mon cher,*" said Mrs. Charbonnier, clasping her hands against her shrunken bosom, "it is the storms in the human breast—the fear, the anger, and the dread—that bring down this kind of illness. It is an illness of the body caused when there is no peace in the spirit." Leif was amazed at what she said. It fit perfectly.

"I wonder all the time why Pa is so angry," said Leif. "He either talks mean or he doesn't talk at all. And whenever he gets a chance, he gets drunk." Maybe he was talking too much. He heaved a sigh. Maybe so, but it felt good to get it out. He leaned forward in his chair and looked at the floor. When he glanced up at the old woman, she held her chin in her hand, curling her forefinger over her lips, nodding.

"You have scar on top of your head." Mrs. Charbonnier reached over and pushed his hair back. "Shape like partridge track. How you get that, *mon cher?*"

"I fell off a wagon when I was little, and the wheel cut my head. A man sewed it together with a needle and thread."

"*Mmm,*" said Mrs. Charbonnier. She was quiet a few moments. "So. Mebbe Papa don't drink the tea. Mebbe he think nothing wrong with him. But you tell him. First, the tea is hops. Hops used to make beer. Tell him it only for men. Second, tell him it calm the stomach when everything going on wrong. Third, it is for you, too, *mon cher.* You try it if Papa don't want it. And if Mama not better by planting time, you bring her to me. Don't wait." Leif stood up and waited quietly in the steady brown-eyed gaze of the old woman.

"Thank you, Mrs. Charbonnier." Leif bowed his head. He had to pick up some things in town and get back home. He was uncertain what to do about paying Mrs. Charbonnier; she had given Ma's ring back. He couldn't use the money he was supposed to buy supplies with, and what he had left of his own was too little. "Mrs. Charbonnier, do you like licorice?"

"Yes, *mon cher.* I love licorice," she said. Leif took the candy from the pouch he'd hung by the door with his jacket and presented it to the old woman.

"It's not much," said Leif, "but next time I come this way I will have more time and bring some tools along."

"Your visit has been my pleasure, *M'sieur* Leif. I hope you will come again. I thank you for clearing the way to my door."

Leif picked up a fifty-pound sack of flour, Pa's tobacco, Ma's cotton thread, a box of Winchester cartridges, and other sundries—including cinnamon. The hide buyer was not around, so he had to take his hides back with him.

Dusk was near. It was time to find shelter. He went to Fischer's Tavern, helped Mr. Fischer once more, and earned another quarter. In the morning, after pancakes and coffee, he headed for home. He hoped Ma's medicine would work. He doubted Pa would take his. But you never knew.

CHAPTER 9

Leif Returns

As Leif trudged off to the north, pulling his loaded toboggan, the tavern talk and Mrs. Charbonnier's words rustled around his ears like leaves in a whirlwind.

To think that Ma had something painful called gallstones because of Pa's rages. It was hard to figure out. At least she wouldn't die. Leif had no idea what made Pa so angry. It was strange to think that Pa's anger came from something. Leif had always thought his face was just made like that—that he was just angry by nature.

"What is wrong with you? Did you think I wouldn't notice?" Pa swung the strap in a powerful arc as Elias covered his head with his arm. "Don't turn away from me," commanded Pa. "I'll teach you to disobey me and then lie about it!"

"Pa, he wasn't home, so I couldn't get it!"

"Don't talk back to me," Pa bellowed. Leif slipped out the door and walked quickly to the barn. Later that night in bed Elias shook silently.

Leif shuddered at the memory. His return path would take him near Anna's lake, where they'd met. He dwelled in the wonder of meeting Anna in the blizzard. "Anna, Anna," he repeated to himself. And then the awe of finding her uncle nearly dead. "Oh, my God," he whispered. He forgot to watch his signs. Twice he had to backtrack to find a marker. He had come to himself, looked about, and didn't know which way to turn. He had to keep his mind in the present moment in these woods. Especially on such an overcast day when he couldn't tell where the sun was.

He shuffled on, pulling the heavy toboggan, alert to the wind and the movements of birds, hares, squirrels, and deer. He focused on his trail markers.

He yearned to see Anna. In Freeport he'd bought more rock candy and licorice and a paper sack of maple candy with the quarter Mr. Fischer had paid him. He'd make a gift of it to her. When he got home he would carve her something.

And he would write her a letter. He'd deliver it himself.

Leif pulled the loaded toboggan through the deep snow, step after step, the snowshoes like the huge footpads of a lynx. He wished he'd coated the bottom of the toboggan with beeswax. Endlessly the wind drifted fallen snow, but no new snow fell. At dusk he found a deep swell on a creek bank and scooped a berth into it. He slept on the hides, wrapped in his buffalo robe.

Late Sunday afternoon he reached the spruce where he had taken shelter with Anna. She was so near, but he could not take time to visit now. He opened up a new entrance to the shallow haven beneath the spruce tree. Charred sticks from the little fire remained. As darkness fell, he ate, then wrapped himself in his robe and drifted to sleep. He dreamed of the partridge, who drummed for his mate.

The next morning Leif shot two large snowshoe hares and a small doe, dressed them out, and laid the limp, steaming carcasses across the load on the toboggan. The hares were fair game, for they were well-adapted to get about in the snow. But taking the doe as she foundered in the bottomless drift was like picking a cabbage. In midafternoon he drew within sight of the farm and quickened his pace. He had a lot of shoveling to do; that was clear.

He'd been gone a day longer than planned. Ma would be worried. If she and Pa hadn't made their way to the barn, the cows couldn't be milked. They'd go dry, and there'd be no more milk and no more cheese to sell until they calved again. Ma could have been stricken with more pains. They might have run out of firewood. Leif shook himself out of his forebodings. He was home now.

He snowshoed up to a pit in front of the barn doors. Pa had managed to get into the barn by re-digging the trench from the house and clearing enough snow to allow one of the doors to swing open. Leif climbed down into the pit and then eased the toboggan down. He pulled the door open and looked into the darkness. "Hey, Pa!"

"Ya!" came Pa's response. Leif stepped inside and made out the form of his father standing in the doorway of the tack room, which was lighted behind him by a small window. Leif noticed Horace lying behind Pa near the stove. Horace rose and trotted to him, grunting softly. Pa frowned at the light shining from the open door behind Leif. "Ya, your ma been worried sick, boy. Better go in right now."

"Hello, old man," he said to Horace, scratching him behind the ears. "I'll talk to you in a little while." He drew the toboggan to the house through the deep slot now partially bridged over with snow. Ma came out on the porch and ran to him, heaving mightily as she threw her arms around him.

She opened the door and waved him in, unable to speak.

After chores, Ma set a steaming kettle of hare and venison stew on the table between them. There were dumplings in it, made from the flour he'd brought. Potatoes and onions had run out. Leif's face was flushed, and his chin and nose tingled. Ma put the soda bread on the table and sat on the bench beside Pa. She heaved a full sigh and bowed her head.

"Thank the good Lord for bringing Leif home safe," she said in a wavering voice. "Pa?" said Ma, inviting him to add a few words.

Pa narrowed his eyes. "Birke, you know I don't follow no high and mighty church authorities and their Bible quotes. I'll not mouth words that don't make no sense to me, no matter what." This was said in a high Swedish lilt.

"Well, that's honest, Bjorn. A man can say the *thanks* that is in his heart anyway." Leif looked up.

"Ya, I'm sure glad to be home. *Jag är glad att jag är hemma,*" he said.

"Amen," said Ma, taking it as a prayer of thanks.

"Ya," said Pa. Leif hung on that brief affirmation.

They spooned stew on their bread while breathing in vapors of wild meat, turnips and parsnips, juniper and sage. The woodstove whistled, spewed, and popped. Time stopped as they took their first swallows of stew and chewed soft dill dumplings. The air was charged with the pale lightning of untold stories.

"So den. How did the trip go?" asked Pa. Leif drew a deep breath. He didn't know what to say first. His eyes flashed up and settled down on the old-world sugar bowl with the blue scroll-work. So Pa was going to listen to him—to Leif!—tell a story about what he had done. He drew a breath.

"Good," said Leif. "Ya, it was good. Did Anna come?"

"Ha! Ha! Ha!" bellowed Pa. "Dere's an Eliasson for you,"

he guffawed. "Ha! Ha! Ha!" Leif looked at his father, and his face flushed.

"The 'burning question,' ya, son?" cackled his father.

"Bjorn," hissed Ma sharply. She looked at him with her lips pressed in a straight line. Her eyes flicked briefly upward. "He conducted himself honorably and did us proud. Yes, Leif, she brought a frozen goose if you can believe! She wouldn't stay but for coffee. Strangest thing—they'd left the head on the goose. She told us quite a story."

"Pretty good on the sliders, too," said Pa. "Not a bad one to latch onto. She'll keep that plow moving right along." He grinned slyly. With that, Leif sensed that he'd been admitted to a mysterious and somewhat wicked brotherhood. One, perhaps, he might not care to join.

"Bjorn, you stop that right now!" Ma stamped her foot and stood up. She stepped over the bench, turned, and stormed out the door, no doubt heading for the outhouse.

"Ah, she'll let off some steam out dere," said Pa in his gravelly voice. Leif started to choke. He got himself under control and focused on the stew. His appetite was huge. They waited for Ma, but events whirled through Leif's mind. Pa had asked him to speak.

"Ya, I heard people talking like I never heard before," said Leif. "The owner of the tavern is German, and the cook is English. I met a Polish lady, and the root lady is French. And I saw the world's ugliest dog."

Ma burst through the door.

"Are you telling stories while I'm outside?" She marched outraged to the table, looking at Leif. Suddenly she plopped a huge ball of snow on Pa's head. Pa's face turned white, then red, and the crack of doom between his eyes turned sideways.

"Aaagghh!" yelled Pa, and he stood up. "What has come over you, Birke? Have you gone daft?"

"I want to hear everything. And would you please show a little respect to your son when he's met a girl. You needn't turn the matter into a wicked joke." Pa rolled his eyes up, puffed out his lips, and blew imaginary steam.

"My turn for a little trip outside," said Leif. He relieved himself in the straw out back and looked up at the stars. The night was still, clear, and cold. The clouds from his breath made colored rings around the moon. He could hear them shouting and carrying on inside.

At the door Leif turned around and looked in the direction of Anna's farm. He would go to see her tomorrow and give her his gifts. He thought of Mr. Fischer's job offer. He could visit Anna from Freeport just as well as from here.

Next morning when Pa was out in the barn, Leif gave the ring back to Ma. "She wouldn't take it," he said. He told Ma the directions for the remedy that Mrs. Charbonnier had given him and showed her the hops tea she had given him for Pa.

"Give me the tea. I'll talk to Pa when the time is right," she said.

"She guessed about Pa's angry spells," said Leif. "The hops is supposed to calm him."

"We'll see."

"I gave her some licorice. It was all I had," said Leif. "I shoveled out the trench to her front door and cleared the snow from around her chimney." Ma nodded at him.

"In the spring when the planting is done, we'll make it good with her," said Ma.

"Ya," said Leif. He was already planning his visit to Anna's.

CHAPTER 10

Visiting Anna

Leif carried the Winchester strapped across his back and a makeshift pack wrapped around his waist as he skied toward Anna's lake. The sun had turned the snowy world scalding bright. He wore wooden slit-goggles so that he could see in the glare. Using the skis saved a lot of time compared to the snowshoes. He didn't have a loaded toboggan to pull on this trip.

The sun would be low when he reached the Sederstrom farm. Now he was about halfway, judging by the time, and he kept a lookout for the brushy area where he had seen the deer on his way to Freeport. When he got into the area, he squatted on his skis among some young fir trees that poked only two or three feet above the snow, and he held the rifle ready. He held still for a quarter of an hour. The fingers on his mittless right hand were growing numb. The cold made him want to move, and finally he leaned forward to stand up. That was when the buck stepped out of the brush, just fifty yards away, and stood almost broadside to him. Leif pressed his cheek against the frigid stock of the rifle, aimed, and brought him down with a shot to the chest behind the front leg. The creature crumpled in the snow as the report rumbled in the air.

The animal was in its second season, not yet full grown, but a good size. Leif moved quickly to dress it out and skin it.

He wanted to arrive at Anna's before dark. He had to work in his shirt with the sleeves rolled up and his hands bared so that he could remove the entrails. Quickly slicing through the belly wall of the animal from sternum to crotch, he rolled the warm, steaming innards out. Rollie and Elias had taught him long ago how to dress a deer. He had no way to store any of the meat away from scavengers, so he had to take with him what he could carry.

The heart and liver he rolled in the powdery snow and left to cool. He freed the hind quarters from the pelvis, sliced the lower legs off at the joints, and rolled the haunches up in the skin. This was the majority of the meat on the deer. Shivering violently, he quickly scrubbed his arms and hands with snow and shook them off. They were still covered with a layer of tallow, but he would have to wash that off with soap and warm water later. He got back into his wool coat, buffalo robe, and mittens, spread the wool blanket from his pack out on the snow, and deposited the tawny hide bundle upon it.

Leif buried the rest of the steaming carcass in the snow, but he didn't expect it would be there on his way back. Wolves or ravens would get it. Or fox or owl. He dropped the snow-frosted heart and liver in the cold pockets of his buffalo robe, grabbed the blanket by its four corners and hoisted it over his shoulder. Now he had a gift not only for Anna but for her whole family.

As Leif approached the farm across the lake, he came first to the barn. Maybe Anna was still doing the evening milking. The sun was low in the west, so when he opened the service door, the light announced him. "Hullo-o-o?" he sang out, so as not to startle the animals.

"Hey!" called a woman's voice behind the cows.

"It's Leif," he called. He didn't know if it was Anna. Could be her mother. He stepped cautiously inside.

"Leif!" Anna stepped into the shaft of light shining from the door, walked quickly forward, grabbed his hand, and gave it a quick squeeze. Her eyes shone. "I've just finished milking," she said. "Come, I'll take you to the house."

Anna took him by the arm, picked up her milk pail, and into the warm farmhouse they went. "Ma—Pa—look who's here. It's Leif!"

"Oh, for heaven's sake," said Mrs. Sederstrom. "Come in, come in," she urged, although he was already quite in. "Set your things down and come sit. So you're Leif! Anna's told us so much about you. I am Gaia." Looking him up and down, she held her hand out to Leif. He propped his rifle beside the door, took Mrs. Sederstrom's hand, and made a quick smiling bow. She was short as Ma but a more ample woman.

"Thank you, ma'am. I'm glad to meet you," said Leif, still holding his bundle in his left hand. His face turned hot, and he grinned shyly. Anna stood aside with a bemused smile and flushed cheeks. Leif glanced about at the sitting room. The wallpaper had broad alternating stripes of white and gray. Delicate bouquets with a touch of green and pink ran on the white. Portraits of relatives hung here and there, and a framed floral design crafted from human hair hung between two candle sconces.

"Welcome, Leif," said Anna's pa, who was tall and thin, the opposite of Leif's father. The top of his head was bald, but his mustache was all the richer for it. "I'm Alder. I'm pleased to meet you," he said with a grin, bobbing his head. "Come and sit by the stove and thaw out for a while." Mr. Sederstrom spoke in a mild and rather musical voice, not at all gruff and gravelly like Leif's pa. He seemed to have made better friends with the English language, too.

"Thank you, sir. Glad to meet you." Leif set the blanket

down, and as soon as he let go of the corners, the deerhide bundle was exposed.

"Looks like you got yourself some venison there," said Mr. Sederstrom.

"Ya, it was very good luck. I got it just the other side of the lake, and you're welcome to it, Mr. Sederstrom," said Leif. "I've got the heart and liver here, too," he said, hauling them out of his buffalo robe pockets.

"Land sakes," said Mrs. Sederstrom. "We can't take all this. You have to take some home to your family, Leif."

These social niceties went back and forth for some time until Leif at last found himself sitting by the stove with a mug of hot coffee, trading small talk with Mr. Sederstrom. Leif talked about his buffalo robe and the anvil, his trip to Freeport, the tavern and Mrs. Charbonnier—although not about the particulars of his mother's ailment, of course. The matter of meeting Anna would keep until later. Meanwhile Anna and her mother got a venison supper ready and called Leif and Mr. Sederstrom to the table.

By now it had gotten dark outside, and Anna had lit the lamps.

Once Leif had gotten some food in his belly, his brain started to work. After supper, he said, "I am very sorry about your brother, Mr. Sederstrom. How is he doing?"

"Ya. You are kind to ask, Leif. It's a pity. He had to have his hands and one foot amputated. And of course his left thighbone was broken. He's in the hospital in Little Falls. Ya, Henrik—he had a hard life."

"Ya, it couldn't be helped," Mrs. Sederstrom agreed, knitting in her rocking chair. "He had a fever in childhood and wasn't right after that."

"Leif," Anna said, "I noticed your hat. It looks like raccoon skins. Can I look at it?" She had hardly spoken since they had met in the barn. Leif lifted the heavy cap off the chair and handed it to Anna.

"You were wearing this . . . " she said slowly.

"Ya, I . . . I was wearing it when I was heading for Freeport." Leif said. "My sister, Ellen, helped me sew the skins together." His face grew warm as he gazed at Anna.

"Your pa must have taught you well for you to know what to do in such a storm," said Mrs. Sederstrom.

"Ya, *tack*. Pa did teach me how to use a shovel."

Mr. Sederstrom swallowed nervously and wiped his mustache.

"So tell me, Leif," said Mrs. Sederstrom, "what possessed you to take Anna under a spruce tree instead of taking her back home?"

"Ma!" Anna cried in horror. Mr. Sederstrom coughed and cleared his throat. Mrs. Sederstrom put her knitting down and stared at Anna with a deep frown.

"No, Anna, I want the straight story from Mr. Eliasson. What is your answer, sir?" Leif was shocked at this hostile question from Mrs. Sederstrom. His mouth went dry, and his palms sweated.

"Mrs. Sederstrom," he said slowly, "Anna was frightened out of her wits and was on her way to the Westrich farm during a terrible blizzard. Something happened to her here, and coming back here was the last thing on her mind."

"I would have died rather than come back here to be further assaulted by that demented, wicked drunk," cried Anna. "I told you all of this! Why do you not believe me?"

"Your mother raises a fair point, Anna," said Mr. Sederstrom.

"Do you have any more to say, Mr. Eliasson?"

Leif spoke slowly, with a dreamlike sense of unreality.

"Anna was dressed in several layers of spring sweaters and a light wool jersey. She was half frozen and could hardly speak. She had broken skies and no poles. It was nearly dark and impossible to see in the blizzard. The only choice we had was to take immediate shelter. To go back—*if* we had made it— might have meant facing Henrik *before* he was disabled by the cow. I helped move him into the house, so I know how big he is. Perhaps if we had tried to go back, you would now have Anna in the hospital missing her hands and a foot." Leif rose slowly to his feet and pressed his palms to his forehead. He spoke with a knot in his throat. "That was the choice we had to make."

Were Mr. and Mrs. Sederstrom now going to throw him out? Anna's face was ashen.

Mr. Sederstrom stood and groaned. He raised his arms like a sleepwalker and approached Leif. He put his hands on Leif's shoulders. "Leif, I believe you. I believe you. I'm sorry." Mr. Sederstrom closed his eyes and took huge breaths. Mrs. Sederstrom stood as well, looking down at the floor and wiping tears. Anna ran to her.

"I believe you both," said Mrs. Sederstrom, embracing Anna.

They were all silent for a long moment, looking down as if in prayer.

"Let's have some cider and apple crisp!" cried Anna.

"I'll get it. Sit down, sit down," said Mrs. Sederstrom.

After everyone had gone to bed, Leif stretched out on a pallet of blankets near the stove. He listened to the sizzling of the coals and the sharp cracks the house made as it contracted in the cold night.

• • •

Quiet sounds of stoking the kitchen stove woke Leif, and he opened his eyes to the yellow light of a single kerosene lamp. "Good morning, Mrs. Sederstrom," he said from the floor by the stove in the sitting room. He sat up on his pallet, yawned and stretched.

"Good morning, Leif. Coffee will be ready soon."

Leif rolled up his buffalo robe and folded the blankets Mrs. Sederstrom had put down for his pallet. Then he removed the ashes from the metal ash box under the stove and laid in more kindling and logs on the glowing embers. Soon Mr. Sederstrom and Anna came in from chores. They'd made it outside somehow without waking him.

After pancakes and coffee, Mr. Sederstrom said to Mrs. Sederstrom, "I'm going to Carl Monson's to talk about spring plowing. I want to break the twelve acres this spring, ya, and that will take his ox team."

"I'll pack some bread and venison for you," said Mrs. Sederstrom, winking at Leif.

"Good, my dear." Mr. Sederstrom gave Leif a grin and stood up.

"Will you take the sleigh?" asked Mrs. Sederstrom.

"Oh, I think not," said Mr. Sederstrom. "That road is far from clear. I'll ride the sliders."

"I'll be heading home myself," said Leif. He rose and shook hands with Mr. Sederstrom.

"You're not leaving just now, are you?" asked Anna. "Won't you have another cup of coffee?" Her cheeks flushed slightly.

"Why, of course!" said Leif, and he sat down again across the table from her. Mrs. Sederstrom poured him another cup of coffee.

"Got to watch those women, Leif," said Mr. Sederstrom with a broad smile. "A man's got to stand up to them!"

"All right," Leif said, holding his mug up to Anna and furrowing his brow. "Just one more cup, and that's it!" They laughed, and Mr. Sederstrom stepped out the door.

"This morning I have a notion to milk both cows by myself, Anna. You stay here and keep Leif's coffee cup filled." Mrs. Sederstrom quickly got into her barn coat and mitts, picked up the milk pails, and stepped outside.

"I guess they mean to leave us alone for a while," said Anna.

"They are very kind," said Leif. "You are lucky to have such parents, even if they do have a little mean streak." They laughed. Leif blinked at Anna for a moment. Then he leaned over the table and kissed Anna's forehead. She sprang up and stepped back.

"Just hold your horses, Mister," she said sternly, her face red. "What do you take me for?" She kissed her thumb, leaned over the table, and pressed it between Leaf's eyebrows. She laughed and ran out onto the porch. Leif followed her, his brain on fire.

"Shall we go for a jaunt, now that we both have skis?" asked Leif.

"Let's save that for when you have to leave," said Anna. "I'll see you across the lake. Come, let's go back inside." When she had closed the door, Anna said, "I'm not an easy woman, but that doesn't mean I don't like you."

"Just because I like you," said Leif, "it doesn't mean I think you're an easy woman."

Anna smiled, and they grasped each other's hands. Her blue eyes lit up Leif's brown ones. Leif blushed and looked down. The partridge track on his head itched madly.

Hours seemed to pass, but in reality it was only seconds. Anna said to Leif while their eyes were locked upon each other, "Leif, let us be friends, kind to each other, no matter what—ya?"

"Ya, that's it. I want that more than anything else. You have said it." Leif's chest flooded with gratitude, and he could not speak any further. He drew a deep breath. He had few enough friends that he could see sometimes. He couldn't travel around as freely as Pa, who had no one to answer to. But now it was different.

"I like your philosophy," said Leif.

"How did you know I had any philosophy?" asked Anna.

"Well, how did you learn to think like you do?" asked Leif.

"I read some of Plato's dialogues of Socrates. I tried to make sense of them, and I thought about myself and my life." Leif was moved to meet someone else who thought so deeply about life.

"Where did you get it?"

"A schoolteacher traveling through stayed with us. I sat up all night reading, and in the morning, he gave me the book."

"Ya. I like what you say. I like doing that, too," said Leif. Anna looked at him. When Leif met her gaze, Anna's whole face—her eyes, her forehead, her cheeks—seemed to be shining on him. That was when Leif felt his heart go up the flue. There it went, and she was the sky it went into.

As if snapping out of a spell, Leif heard himself say, "I read about the electric light invention in *Popular Science Monthly*. I would like to see how it works. Electricity is supposed to be like the sparks you get from rubbing wool with a piece of amber, and they make it somehow go through a wire."

Anna eyebrows rose. "I read in the Little Falls newspaper that an electric torch will be mounted at the Hennepin Bridge in Minneapolis. That will be a sight to see! Leif, what do you think about . . . about God?"

Leif looked off into the distance.

"I don't believe everything the preachers say," he said.

"What do you believe?"

"I don't know. I have lots of questions. But I still pray."

"Ya, I do, too," said Anna.

"I believe in treating others as you want them to treat you."

"It's simple, and it's everything."

"I like singing, and I like sitting in the willow tree by the creek. Have you read Mark Twain?" Leif asked.

"Just the first half of *The Adventures of Tom Sawyer.* The rest was missing."

"How did you get it?"

"Pa made shoes for Olga Forstrom. She's a widow with three children. And she gave him four books—well, three and a half. Pa didn't want to take them, but he said that Olga would keep her dignity if he accepted them, so he did."

"What were the other books? Oh, never mind! I can't ask that." Leif thought it amounted to asking to borrow them.

"Of course you can. They are *Eight Cousins* by Louisa May Alcott, *Around the World in Eighty Days* by Jules Verne, and *The Man Without a Country* by Edward Hale. You can borrow them if you like. I've read them all, and they are very good."

"Can I see *The Man Without a Country?*" asked Leif. Something about the idea of a man without a country spoke to him. Sometimes he felt as if he didn't have a place he belonged. Maybe the book would give him a hint of how to find it.

Anna took the book from a small stand near the sitting room window and laid it in front of Leif. The cover was dark orange like a maple leaf in fall and worn to yellow on the corners. The title was embossed in gold. "Thank you, Anna. Now daylight is burning, and I must go back."

"Take the rest of the venison to your ma and pa," said Anna.

"You keep the heart and liver, and I'll take the rest," replied Leif. "Some of the meat is buried on the other side of the lake. If anything remains of it, I'll get that, too." Leif rolled his portion of deer meat in the stiff hide and set it upon the blanket. Out on the porch, Anna clamped her boots onto her sliders, and Leif did the same.

Leif and Anna crossed the lake. When they reached the western shore, they stood for a moment hand in hand. When Leif leaned toward her, Anna turned her cheek to him. He kissed her there and inhaled deeply.

"Good-bye for a little while," said Leif.

"Come again soon?" asked Anna, blushing a little.

"Ya, as soon as I can. See this old willow tree?" He skied to it. "There is a hollow here," he said, showing her a large hole where a branch must have broken off long ago. "Maybe sometime when I cannot stop I will leave a letter there. I will drum on the tree with sticks and return home."

Anna put her mittened hand into the hole. "Perhaps you'll find a letter from me. Be sure to check."

Leif grinned and skied a few yards away.

"I'll bring you the whole *Tom Sawyer.*"

Anna waved, and they turned toward their homes. Leif wore a smile until he reached the dark woods, and then he broke into loud singing.

CHAPTER 11

Facing Pa

Two weeks later, on a Sunday well before dawn, Leif left the farm on his skis with *Tom Sawyer* and a letter. When he reached the message tree by Anna's lake, he looked into the hole and saw something. It was a note from Anna.

> *Dear Leif,*
> *Hello. Here's a little something to remember me by.*
> *I like to carve little things.*
> *Yours truly, Anna.*

He looked in the hole again, took off his mitt, reached in, and pulled out a small wooden medallion that just fit in the palm of his hand. One side was fashioned like a sun with undulating rays flowing outward from the center. On the other side was carved "Anna." A keepsake from Anna. Leif admired her fine carving skills.

He had not brought a pencil along, so he could not leave a note to thank Anna for her gift. He left his letter and the book, which was wrapped in a piece of oilskin he'd found in the loft of the barn, and he drummed on the tree. But the sound didn't carry. It was like beating on a stiff rope. Leif searched until he found an old beech that had died and gone hollow and fallen against another tree. The barkless old leaner gave a resonant sound that carried far, and Leif drummed rapidly, like a partridge.

There was no time to stop, no time to rest and visit. Ma was spending the night with a pregnant neighbor, and Leif had to be home in the morning to do chores. He carried the medallion inside his mitt, felt it against the back of his hand as he grasped the ski pole. He skied back with great energy.

Leif returned home near midnight. He entered the house quietly, but Pa still got up to carp at him. "So den. Do you think you can just take a day off any time you like? Do you think I might having something to say about it? Who do you think you are, den? Answer me."

Leif looked at his father.

"I went to leave a letter for Anna. . . ."

"I don't care what you went for. I run this house, and I say when you can go and come."

Leif met his father's angry gaze.

"I will visit Anna. . . ."

"Don't tell me what you will do."

"You told me to answer you, and this is my answer. . . ."

Pa's eyes narrowed. He clenched his fists and took a step toward Leif.

"Who do you think you are?" he hissed, stabbing his finger at him. Pa then turned his rumpled self around and went back to bed, not waiting for Leif to answer. Leif's heart sank.

Never mind that it was a Sunday. Never mind that it was the middle of winter, when they often sat around the stove whittling for lack of anything better to do. Everything that could be sharpened was sharpened twice over.

Leif supposed that when he was gone Pa had to help Ma.

And Ma had to help Pa. Leif could only shake his head. He had a right to go see his sweetheart once in a while.

But Leif was troubled. Jesus had said of the commandment not to kill that while he who kills shall be liable for judgment, so shall he who is angry with his brother be in danger of the judgment. So, Leif concluded, it would be better if he told his pa in a kind way that he intended to go visit Anna, so as not to provoke his pa to anger and put him in danger of the judgment.

Finding the courage to speak such a thing to Pa was another matter. For when the occasion arose, Leif found his tongue glued to the roof of his mouth. He could not move his jaw on such an errand any more than he could walk through a six-foot snowdrift on his hands. He would not listen to his father say yes or no to whether he could go see Anna. That was his decision. Besides, Pa did not allow Leif to tell him anything, whether in a kind way or not. Nor did Pa offer any reasons for his judgments on what Leif did.

Leif spoke to Pa only when necessary, and Leif had not much to discuss with Ma. The winter had become very, very old and stiff.

The following Saturday evening, before Pa even went to bed, Leif stood at the end of the plank table and began packing his small rucksack right out in the open for a trip to see Anna. He had had enough of evading Pa. Now Pa would have a clear chance to give his reasons for saying no.

Pa sat near a lamp with a board in his lap, cutting a pair of shoe soles from a thick piece of leather. "What do my eyes tell me now?" said Pa with mock innocence. "Is Leif going off again to visit his sweet muffin?" Leif quivered but ignored him and put a couple of books in his sack, considering whether to add a third. "What?" snapped Pa. "You will now ignore your pa when he speaks to you?"

"Sounded to me like he was speaking to himself," said Leif, tossing his comb in the sack. "And he wasn't far off the truth."

"You dare to mock me!" roared Pa, gripping his cutting board with both hands. Leif turned and faced Pa.

"No, Pa, I am asking for a little respect."

"Respect? I'll teach you respect!" Pa stood up, and the board, leather, and knife all went sprawling. He came straight for Leif. Leif ducked low and caught Pa's thighs with his shoulder. Pa folded and fell over him. Leif fell face-down on the floor, twisted himself out from under Pa like a greased pig, and stood up ready for more. Leif was ready to fight, and he knew Pa could take him apart.

But Ma planted herself between them. She spoke through her teeth. "This has gone far enough." Ma weighed less than either of them, but there was steel in her voice, and she commanded the room. Pa grunted.

"Saved again, eh, Leif?" Pa huffed and snorted and worked himself to his feet, doubled over more than a little. "When you hit a man low down like that, you better be ready to finish it."

"I'm ready, Pa." Leif felt strangely calm now, though he trembled and his belly heaved.

Ma shoved her palm into Leif's chest like an iron poker and made him step back.

"That's enough. What are you, a couple of schoolboys? Do I have to ship you both off to the county children's home?" Leif felt ashamed, and Pa was looking at the floor, too. Ma looked from one to the other. "Leif, I think you ought to sleep in the hayloft tonight."

Horace heaved himself to his feet as Leif walked up to his pen. "My friend," said Leif, "I am bruised." He touched the place on his forehead and cheek where he'd hit the floor. Leif felt how his shoulder was numb. Horace sniffed the air, and Leif stroked his snout and his ears. "But I think I'll live."

As he made a bed in the hay and spread out his blankets, he wondered if anything had been settled. Maybe. At least Pa knew now that he wasn't going to back down, that he was ready to stand up for himself. And if Pa wanted to make life impossible for him, Leif could go to Freeport and accept Mr. Fischer's offer of a job.

In the morning Leif was dressed, gingerly stretching his sore shoulder, when Ma came into the barn with the milking pails. "Morning, Ma."

"Good morning, Leif. Oh, you got a nice shiner there. How you going to explain that to Anna?"

"For true? A shiner?" He gently probed around his eye and felt the puffiness. It must have happened when he hit the floor. Anna would want him to explain it, of course. And her parents would wonder, too. "Maybe I got to leave a note for her this time. And I really wanted to see her. Maybe I could tell her . . ."

"What—that you fell off your horse? That you took a header out of the hayloft? Leif, don't be making up lies to cover the truth. That's a coward's way to live, for sure. But you could say that you fell on the floor."

"Oh, Ma, that's a big help."

Each of them took a stool and a pail and started milking.

"You got to stick with the truth, son. Though if it isn't asked for, you can leave some of it out." She had an impish tone in her voice. "Leif, sooner or later Anna is going to know that you got trouble with your father. You can't just throw some wallpaper over that knothole." Leif frowned and was quiet.

"How's Pa looking this morning?"

"He's not used to falling on the floor either. He's moving

| 81 |

around a little stiffer than usual. But he's not in a bad mood. You could go in." Leif pulled one corner of his mouth back. He might as well. Nothing like a shiner to spark some respect from another fellow.

Leif went in when he was done with the animals. Pa didn't talk to him or look at him and shortly went out to the barn. In the mirror it wasn't such a big shiner, but it was enough to notice. Leif ate his breakfast, took up his rucksack and the Winchester, and headed for Anna's on his skis. He'd decide when he got to the lake whether he'd go up to the farmhouse or leave a note in the tree.

CHAPTER 12

A Talk with Anna

"I'll tell you all about it," Leif said, grinning at Anna's puzzled expression as she stood near the front door. "Can we ski to the lake?"

"Sure, it's Sunday. It's allowed," said Anna, smiling back. She invited him in for a mug of milk and some hot *lefsa* with butter and sugar. They thanked each other for the gifts they had exchanged in the willow tree. After Leif was rested and warmed up, Anna got her skis, and they headed for the lake.

"I've been waiting for a chance to talk with you, Anna. I got worried that with all the terrible things that happened when we met, and the questions your parents had when I came to visit, that maybe you would rather forget everything and not be bothered with me."

Anna stopped in her tracks.

"Leif Eliasson! What nonsense is this? It was I who brought all the calamity upon you. It would be you who would be completely justified if you never wanted to see me again."

Leif looked at her.

"It's not whose fault anything is. It's just that everything is so mixed up, the good and the bad. And the good is very good, and the bad is very bad." Leif stopped in his tracks. "I'm very happy to hear what you just said."

"*Tack så mycket.* Thanks so much. Ya, it has been a hard time. Pa got word that Henrik is not expected to live much longer, so he has gone to Little Falls to be with him."

"Oh, I am sorry."

"*Tack.*" Thanks, Leif.

Just then Mrs. Sederstrom passed by them on her way to the barn.

"You two had better move along. It's going to get dark before you make it past the barn."

They started skiing again.

"I remember when we were children," said Anna, "and Henrik would pretend he was a horse. We would ride him around, and he would rear up and try to buck us off. He was always making fun with us kids."

Leif considered her story for a few moments.

"Anna," he said, "I have only your stories to know Henrik. There is both love and fear in them."

"Ya, it's true. Poor man. Something happened to him in childhood that made him not right in the head."

Leif reached under his cap to rub his scar.

"Ya, so your ma said. He had a fever."

Anna looked at him.

"Ya. I don't know any more than that. Pa don't talk about old times much."

"Mine don't either," said Leif. They stood in silence. "But Henrik loved you and you loved him, so he wasn't just a monster or a madman."

"Ya, for true. Then maybe we all got a little monster in us, too," said Anna.

They looked into the snow and then skied slowly on toward the lake, nearing the steep slope.

"Anna, I don't get to visit as often as I would like. My Pa is not easy. He's not a very happy man."

"Is this about your eye?"

Leif heaved a deep sigh.

"Ya."

"Did he smack you?"

"No. But we did have a little disagreement last night."

"A disagreement?"

"All right, this is the story. My pa thinks he controls every breath I take. I have to ask permission to do everything I do that isn't work. Here it is, late February, middle of winter, when people sit around and carve and knit for lack of any work to do. Everything has been repaired. All the blades have been sharpened."

"And it's Saturday evening? Last night?" asked Anna.

"Yes, last night. I began packing my kit on the table in front of Ma and Pa, preparing to come visit you. Pa became angry because I had not asked permission. He spoke to me in a mean and sarcastic way, as if I were a little boy, and I told him I would like to be treated with respect. So he says, 'Respect? I'll teach you respect.' Then he charged at me, and I ducked down, and he fell on top of me. I hit the floor, and that's how I got my shiner."

"That was the end of it?"

"Ma put a stop to it, or he would have blackened the other eye. You saw him. He's built like a bear and has a temper to match. Ma told me I better sleep in the hayloft, so I did. I talked to Horace for a while. At least he listens. In the morning Pa didn't say a word to me."

Anna blew a breath out.

"Who's Horace?"

"My pet pig. I got him right after I fell out of the wagon. Ma brought him home from an auction she and Pa went to. He was sick, and I fed him from a bottle. He got well, and he's been my friend for thirteen years."

They stood now at the top of the slope, looking out across the lake at the sunset.

Leif heaved a sigh.

"I want to be a farmer. I think it suits me. It's what I want to do. My brothers have left, so I stand to take over the farm. But working with Pa . . . I don't know."

Anna shoved off and skied down the slope. Leif followed, and they skied out on the lake for a while.

"Sounds to me like you've got a tough job to work things out with your pa," said Anna.

"Ya. That's for sure." He looked at Anna. Suddenly the stakes seemed very high. He felt a knot in his stomach.

Anna stopped and turned to him.

"I'm a farmer at heart, too. So I understand, and I do so wish you the best of luck. You deserve it." Anna looked at him earnestly.

They dropped their ski poles and embraced, pressing their cheeks together. Leif kissed Anna on the temple. She pushed back a little, and then they shared their first proper kiss.

"Anna, Anna, I will do everything I can to find peace with Pa. Somewhere inside he's got to want to find peace, too."

"God help you both, Leif."

"Anna! Leif! Come to supper!" Mrs. Sederstrom called.

Leif and Anna laughed, turned their skis around, and went in.

CHAPTER 13

Another Side of Ma, April 1881

It was Tuesday, the second week of April, and the temperature had risen into the forties. Leif was going to take Ma into Upsala in the grain wagon if they could get through the mud. Helmuth, a neighbor, said a supply wagon had made it to the store in town.

Snow cover, once so mighty and deep, had slumped and taken on a glaze. Rivulets invaded the tunnels of shrews and field mice as melt percolated downward and flowed along the ground. Birds sang as if encouraging the meadows to come into flower. Ragged, slanting shafts appeared in the drifts where the sun had found some stain or dimple in which to concentrate its rays.

Ducks and geese flew honking and squeaking overhead, chattering as if amazed at the winter that had held the north land in its grip. Cardinals, blue jays, chickadees, and finches added to the wild chorus.

"What's that bright blue one, Ma?" Leif asked, pointing toward the leafless wild plum tree just east of the house where a bird of royal azure perched.

"Indigo bunting," she said. "A little early for him." When the mourning doves appeared, Leif had grabbed the shotgun, but the snow then had been too deep to allow pursuit. His mouth had watered for a taste of dove breast.

Ma climbed up on the seat, and Leif clucked the team into action. "Gyup."

What Leif loved most about the thaw was that the sweet and pungent fragrances of barn, earth, and trees had returned to the air. Day by day, the depth of the snow cover diminished and the rivers rose. The creek had risen far above its banks. Open water appeared, black against the snow. The horses cavorted in bursts of devilment, rolled in the slush, then shook it off. Even the cows gathered outside, bobbed their heads, uttered their mournful glissandos, and lashed their tails with anticipation of sweet grasses to come.

On the roads, slush and mud filled the ruts between the snowbanks, but the communal pulse quickened nevertheless. People came alive, knowing that soon they'd be drinking coffee with neighbors who'd been cut off from them for months.

Truth be told, as Ma confessed to Leif once they were underway, her need to go to town was aimed as much at meeting folks and trading news as buying groceries.

Leif steered the wagon into the firmest-looking parts of the slushy road, but the wagon threatened to bog down again and again. He said to Ma, "I'm starting to wish I'd hitched up all four instead of just Star and Maggie." They made it most of the way up a slope when the wagon became hopelessly mired.

"I can't push 'em any harder," Leif said. "We might as well sit here a while and let them rest. If they can't pull us out, I might have to walk back and get the other horses."

"Leif, another reason I wanted to make this trip is to talk to you about Pa." She looked him in the eyes. "I didn't want him walking in on us. I know how he calls you a mama's boy whenever I have to step in."

"Okay, Ma," said Leif. "We got some time now." The sun

was bright and the breeze was gentle, so it was not unpleasant sitting a spell.

"Leif, don't think I don't know what you're going through. I'm glad you've met Anna. She seems like a very smart and able woman. You've got every right to court her and go visit her on Sundays."

Leif nodded and sat up straighter.

"Thanks, Ma."

"You just got to know, Leif, your Pa needs to think he's in control. You can't take him head-on. But it's good you stood up to him last Saturday. I swear, I nearly laughed out loud," she chuckled. "You showed him that you are willing to stand up for yourself. You just need to work on your . . . your polish. Your tactics."

"Ma, I'm not going to let him say that I can't go when I want to go see Anna, and there isn't a reason in the world not to."

"That's not what I'm talking about, honey. You know what diplomacy is? It's the art of saying and getting things in a way that allows the other person to save face. You know what I mean?"

Leif was puzzled.

"Now that you've shown Pa how fixed you are on courting Anna, and you've stood up for yourself, all he needs is for you to let him know that that's what you're gonna do tomorrow—*if he don't mind*. Throw in some little thing that makes it look like you mean to abide by his say, but make it clear what you want to do. I'm wagering that he will go along."

"Well, I guess I know what you mean, Ma. But I am not going to abide by his say if he says no."

"Ya, Leif, I understand. Again, that's not the point. We both know that you are going to go ahead and make your visit. But if you can give Pa a little bit of a grip, he most likely will go along. It's better that way than getting crossways with him when you don't need to. You might have to give a little like that in order to get more in the long run. *Förstår du?*"

"Ya, I get your drift." Leif sat with this notion in silence. He pushed his stocking cap awry on his head. It was really quite warm.

"You think these horses are ready to pull us to town?" Ma asked.

"We'll see." Leif sent a mighty roll down the reins and shouted, "Gyup! Hyah! Hyah! Let's go, Star! Let's go, Maggie! C'mon! Take us to town!" Maggie and Star leaped forward. The wagon oozed forth, and gradually they pulled up to higher ground. The road leveled off, and they were on their way again. They had a half mile to go before they hit the streets of Upsala and the mire produced by a swarm of wagons. The horses leaned into their harness.

"Leif, let me say something else before we get in with a bunch of folks. Your pa knows that you are his last hope to keep the farm in this family. So you got that to work with. You just need to use what?"

"Diplomacy."

"Attaboy!" Ma slapped him on the thigh, and Leif grinned. He hadn't seen quite this side of his ma before. He steered the wagon slowly into the muddy arena surrounding the store. Ya, so maybe a little diplomacy would ease Pa out of his own mud when it came to visiting Anna, but there was more at stake.

CHAPTER 14
Ellen's Visit, June 1881

Leif harnessed Star and Maggie to the grain wagon and whistled for Belka. The dog jumped up on the seat beside him. "Gyup," said Leif, and they headed south for Albany, where Ellen would arrive at the train station. Ellen was six years older than Leif. She had changed since she had started working in Minneapolis, but she was still herself. She worked as a housekeeper and nanny for the Woodhouse family. She had a level head and a cheerful heart and had given wise counsel to Leif all his life. He was eager to see her.

Birds exploded out of the weeds in front of the wagon, and the horses jumped. "Easy. It's just some partridges," he said. "Easy, whoa."

Leif drove into Albany a little after three o'clock. He tied the rig to a rail behind the depot, walked around the small wooden building, and sat on a bench in the sun, facing the tracks. He made Belka lie down beside him. Several ricks of firewood awaited the train. Soon the stationmaster walked out of the depot and looked at his pocket watch.

"Warm one today, id'n it?" He wiped his face with a blue bandana, lifted his cap, and pulled it back down on his curly black-and-silver hair. He wore spectacles with round lenses, and he had gray fuzz in his ruddy ears. Leif stared at the man and thought of Mrs. Charbonnier.

"Yes, sir. Sure is." Leif smiled at the man. "How long till the train comes, sir?"

"Oh, shouldn't be 'nother ten, fifteen minutes or so." He spat into a bush. "Son, if you want to be the first to know when the train is coming, you put your ear to the rail, and you'll hear it." The man spat another streak of tobacco juice and went back inside. As he turned, Leif noticed a pin on his coat that read "Crawford."

Leif was curious to see if sound would indeed travel through the rail, but the instant he laid his ear down on the track—ay!—he jerked back. In the sun the rail had gotten hot as a fry pan. Just then he heard ringing iron and looked down the tracks to see a gang of lusty men hammering spikes. Leif pulled his cap down and trotted toward the workers to see what they were doing. Belka loped alongside him, his tongue trailing like pink smoke.

When Leif got within earshot, he heard talk so salty, it made the Freeport tavern sound like Sunday school. Four shovels dug down on both sides of a tie. Men stood up on the shovels and chanted while rocking them back and forth.

I don't know but I've been told.
Susie has a jelly roll.
I don't know . . . huh.
But I've been told . . . huh.
Susie has . . . huh
A jelly roll . . . huh.

Each time they yelled "huh," they all got up on their shovels and rocked them back. He watched this odd dance briefly and then returned to the station. The train might pull in any minute. He stood rocking and humming under his breath.

When Leif sat back down on the bench at the depot building, Mr. Crawford appeared again. "Tie gang," he said, working a plug of tobacco in his teeth. "Flood washed out the ballast. Get up on them shovels and rock and sing. It's called "gandy-dancin'." Creep that ballast under the tie. Give it a good bed. Burn your ears? Ha! Ha!" The swarthy-faced station master walked away. Leif grinned sheepishly after him and tugged on his cap.

A few minutes later, Leif placed his leather cap on the rail and pressed his ear against it. He heard a pulsing, windlike sound. Surely it was the train. He looked a half mile up the line where the tracks came out of the trees, and a few minutes later the engine came into view, its whistle wailing and smoke pouring from the big funnel. The huge black locomotive pulled into the station, filling the air with woodsmoke and the rumble of its engine.

Brakes squealed, and the train churned to a stop. The engine blew off a great cloud of steam with a loud hiss. Two—no, four—wheels behind the engine were about as tall as Leif was. Fancy gold letters on the engine read "St. Paul, Minneapolis and Manitoba Railway Co." Behind the engine a car carried firewood for the locomotive's boiler. Following that car was a mail car, two passenger cars, two freight cars, and a caboose. It was a short train on new track.

Leif shifted from foot to foot, trying to guess which car Ellen was on. Then a railroad man stepped off the second passenger car, turned, and helped a short, stout figure step off the car with her bag. "Ellen!" called Leif, waving his cap.

They ran toward each other and hugged each other tightly, Ellen laughing heartily. Leif loved that laugh. "I'm glad you're here!" Leif whispered, blinking back his tears. Leif hadn't realized he missed his older sister so much. It was embarrassing to be seized with such strong emotions in public in broad daylight.

"And I'm so glad to be here, Leif. Look how tall you are!" she said, gripping her grinning brother by the shoulders. "You've become a man!"

He blushed. Ellen always had a way of making him feel good. Within a heartbeat she took his left hand and raised it over her head, turning a pirouette. She then grabbed his other hand, spun him around, laughing, forcing him to dance a jig with her. It was true—she was now a foot shorter than he. She was short and round, but she could dance nimbly as an elf. Her large head looked like an elf's, too. She had Pa's ice-gray eyes, but in her face they were large and merry as the summer sky.

"Let's get some root beer," she said. "Look, there's Solly's. They have root beer. I'll buy." She took his elbow as if he were her beau, only she was doing the steering. They walked around the depot and across the street and mounted the boardwalk in front of the bank. All the stores faced the tracks across the main street in town. Only the depot, a water tank, its windmill, and an icehouse sat across the street next to the tracks. The water tank was used to fill the engine's boiler, and the icehouse held large cakes of lake ice cut in the winter and packed in sawdust. It was used to cool perishables from the farms bound for the city—especially butter, milk, and eggs.

Next to the bank was Solly's General Store, and O'Toole's Livery sat on the other side of Solly's. Ellen bought them mugs of root beer and a couple of graham crackers for a total of eight cents, and they stood in the shade on the covered boardwalk. Both of them had had enough of sitting.

"Mmm. Solly's root beer is the best," said Ellen. "Better than any I've tasted in the city. I think he puts an extra touch of ginger in it."

"It's sweet and wet," said Leif, wiping the froth from his upper lip.

"Oh, piffle, Leif. You sound like Pa," said Ellen, munching a bite of graham cracker.

"It's the only root beer I ever had, Ellen. It just tastes like root beer. It's good. At least it's not as bitter as that dandelion root stuff that Rollie used to make."

"Yes, I remember that!" Ellen said and laughed.

Ellen took her hat off and fanned herself. "Oh, Leif," she said, "look. A burning cinder from the firebox flew in the window and nearly set my hat on fire. Look at that hole! Another passenger noticed smoke coming from it. Can you imagine? I'll have to sew a flower over it." She handed the hat to Leif.

"Hmm," said Leif. "Why didn't you just close the window?"

"And suffocate? It was hot enough to melt your buttons, I tell you. Next time I come in the spring or fall—never again summer."

"How long was the trip, Ellen? Didn't you enjoy it at all?" Leif couldn't fathom anything more exciting than riding on a train—something he'd never done in his life.

"Six hours it was, Leif. And yes, I did enjoy it—mostly. It was very interesting looking at the lakes and trees along the way. First there were houses and buildings, then lakes and trees. Of course, there were also trees and lakes, and then woods and a few large ponds here and there."

Leif tried to imagine the houses and buildings.

"The towns were interesting, but one was pretty much like the next: some had a depot, and some didn't. Sometimes they just put off the mail and took on mail. In Elk River they unloaded a piano. Whenever people boarded, I looked to see what kinds of things they were carrying, what they were wearing, their hats, and so forth."

"You must have gotten awful hungry," said Leif. Six hours to go a hundred miles. Why, that amounted to sixteen miles per hour—about as fast as a horse running at top speed. Of course, the train made stops along the way, so it had to go faster than that in between towns. Leif shook his head. It must be hard to even breathe at that speed.

"Well, I had some apples and biscuits, so I didn't starve," said Ellen. "I tell you, it will be a good thing when they do away with these outdated wood-burning locomotives, Leif, and get the modern coal burners. Why, those cinders could set the whole train on fire!"

Leif set his mug on the bench.

"That was good, Ellen. When you are done, we can get going." The North Two River was a four-hour drive. They would make camp there, have enough time to catch some fish, eat their supper, and settle themselves for the night. It would be good to sit by the fire with Ellen. She understood how it was with Pa.

Ellen drained her mug and set it beside Leif's.

"All right, brother. Let's go!"

CHAPTER 15

Revelations

Ellen closed her eyes now and then while the horses plodded and the wagon creaked. She took a deep breath and released it with a hum of delight. "Oh, the air is so pure and sweet out here," she said. "City air is full of dust and smoke."

Leif was quiet, too. He glanced at Ellen. She had been a rock and a guide all his life, a second mother. Once, their gazes met and they laughed, clutched hands, and harked back to the days long ago when they had played together as children.

They arrived at the North Two River not far upstream of its mouth on Two River Lake. Leif unharnessed the horses and let them graze free. They would not stray far. Belka would bring them back if they did wander off.

While Leif fished amid the weeds and rocks in the sandy-bottomed river, Ellen scouted in the woods along the bank and found some chanterelle mushrooms and lamb's quarters. She made a campfire, and when Leif carried a couple of pickerel up from the river, they roasted the fish on sticks and boiled the mushrooms and greens with the potatoes Leif had brought along.

As the western sky grew orange and the brightest stars appeared, Leif and Ellen ate their dinner and peeled back the first layers of their recent lives.

Maggie and Star, mother and daughter, stood with heads

hanging between Leif and Ellen, eyes half-closed, seeming to enjoy the conversation. After a time Maggie lay down flat on the ground, and within a few minutes she began to snore. Ellen raised her eyebrows at Leif, glancing toward the horse. Leif shrugged. "She must have stayed awake all the time you were gone, Ellen, and now she is catching up on her sleep."

Ellen rolled her eyes and released a deep chuckle. "Oh, for heaven's sake, Leif." Star nuzzled Maggie, and the older horse got to her feet again.

"So the Woodhouses went away on a trip?" asked Leif.

"Ya, they go every year to Pennsylvania, to a big meeting of their religious society."

"Do you go to their church?"

"Ya, to mind the children. But it suits me. They have no minister. Everyone sits in silence until the Spirit moves one of them, man or woman, to speak."

"Never heard of such a thing," said Leif.

"Mrs. Woodhouse works for the right of women to vote," said Ellen. "They allow me to borrow books from their library, and I help the children with their studies. I am learning as much as the children. I am lucky to work for them.

"But tell me, Leif, how is it for you, home alone with Pa and Ma?"

"Oh, it's the same as usual. . . ."

"Pa still . . ."

"Ya, he's never happy with anything I do. I think I might go to work in Freeport. The tavern owner offered me a job."

"Oh, Leif. That's too bad." The air had grown still, and mosquitoes hummed around them. Leif was ready to burst with his news.

"Ellen, I met a girl."

"Leif, why didn't you tell me?"

"But I'm telling you now, Ellen."

"Well, then, what is her name? Tell me all about her." Ellen seized Leif by the arm.

Leif told Ellen how he met Anna in the blizzard in January, how he made a shelter for them under the tree—and about Uncle Henrik. He told her how Pa always growled and carped at him when he took a Sunday off now and then to go visit Anna. "You would think I had betrayed the farm to the devil," he said. "He wants to control my every move."

"Sounds like Pa," said Ellen.

"A few weeks ago I found a little broken-down shay and brought it home. It needs a wheel, and the axle is cracked. The canopy is banged up. I can make it like new and take it to see Anna. But every time I spend a little time on it, Pa flays me alive."

Leif told Ellen about his meeting with Mrs. Charbonnier. "Of course, Pa refused to drink the tea. I tried it, and it was bitter. I put some honey in it."

"Ya, Ma wrote me about all of that. She said her remedy must have worked. She hasn't had any pains for a month—at least as of when she wrote in April."

"Oh, that's good. She never said anything to me."

"Did you ask?"

"No, I thought it was none of my business."

"Oh, you men. See, you are getting to be just like Pa."

"Ellen, don't say that. She's my ma. I can't just ask about her private affairs."

"I suppose you're right, Leif. But you could ask about that, since she had you get the medicine and all. You could just say,

'How's the old gallbladder doing, Ma?'"

"Ha, ha! You are too much, Ellen."

They talked by the fire as the light in the west went from orange to lavender to dusky blue, and bats darted overhead chasing mosquitoes. Finally darkness took over, and thousands of stars speckled the sky. The campfire burned down to red embers, and they talked on. Frogs and crickets set up curtains of trills and chirps that pulsed in the dark. The air grew cool. "Ready to turn in, Leif?" asked Ellen.

"Ya," said Leif, stretching.

They spread the wagon box cover on the grassy riverbank, rolled up in their blankets, and pulled the edges of the canvas cover over themselves. The river burbled over its stones, and the breath of grasses and trees cooled into delicate fog that curled like mare's tails upon the ground.

Leif stirred eggs and potatoes in the pan over a small fire. Ellen turned under the tarp and groaned.

"Are you ready for some breakfast, Ellen?"

"Oh, yes, Leif, I can't lie abed all day. Mmm. I haven't slept under the stars in ages."

"Pretty soon the sun will be roasting you."

"Go away, Belka!" said Ellen. "You've rolled in something dead."

"Maybe the fish guts I left on the rocks."

Soon Leif and Ellen were driving again, and Belka trotted alongside. They crossed the river at the Peterson Bridge and followed a trail along the bank for seven miles to the place where the Olds Bridge was out, and then they followed the wagon road toward Upsala.

Ellen and Leif rode in silence for a while that morning. The wagon wheels chirped, the wagon box creaked on its springs, hooves plodded, harnesses rustled. The tangy aroma of horse sweat twined with the scent of sun-heated grasses, and dragonflies flashed their colors. Grasshoppers and cicadas snapped and buzzed; robins and warblers filled the air with a filigree of sound. Wild blooms abounded, especially coneflowers, daisies, and wild sweet peas. The floods of the spring had left so much moisture in the ground that everything was green though little rain had fallen since early May.

"Leif. You still must tell me about Anna!"

So Leif told her more about Uncle Henrik and the response of Anna's pa and ma when he began telling them how his and Anna's paths had first crossed.

"Oh, Leif. That's all very interesting, but don't just talk about things that happened. Tell me what Anna herself is like!"

Leif looked at her, nodded, and stared ahead for a few moments.

"She's kind and witty. She has a keen mind and tells good jokes. Such expressions she makes! Her hair is like ripe wheat. Her eyes are blue as an indigo bunting. She has four older brothers, so she knows how to handle herself around fellows. She knows her own mind, I'll tell you. And she loves to read as much as I do, Ellen. She is an expert carver. Maybe somehow you can meet her. She came to check on Ma and Pa before I got back from Freeport."

"Good, Leif. Anything else?"

"She . . . we like to talk about running a farm. But it would have to be our farm. Two of her brothers are still home. So it's about Pa, Ellen. How can I ever work with him?"

"Will he ever treat you as an equal and trust you?" Ellen asked. "Leif, I've been thinking what a shame it would be if you also leave the farm and none of us take it over. I wouldn't blame you at all for leaving. I know how Pa is. Let's stop for a while, let the horses rest."

"Sure. It's about time." Leif pulled the reins back. "Whoa," he called to Maggie and Star. He jumped down and hung a feed bag with a few handfuls of oats on each horse. He walked away from the wagon a few paces and gave a sharp tweet on the whistle to call Belka out of the woods.

Ellen climbed down and sat in the grass under an oak tree beside the wagon track. Leif could see that she had more on her mind. "Look, here's an old wagon track going off to the east," she said. "I wonder where it goes?"

"Oh, it goes to the old Hilgendorf farm. That's where I found the broken-down shay and the anvil that I traded for my buffalo robe. No buildings left—just a caved-in root cellar and some foundation stones."

"Somebody might have taken the buildings apart to salvage the lumber," Ellen said.

"Or burned them for the nails," said Leif.

They shared water from a crockery jug.

Leif sighed.

"I don't know what to do. I'm scared that Anna won't stick with me if I don't take the farm. She is not a town kind of girl. And I can't do it if Pa won't . . ."

"Ya, I think Pa . . . is squeezing his hope to death."

Leif looked at her.

"What do you mean?"

"I don't know. I've been away a few years, and when I look back, it seems like Pa has always tried to steer everybody down a straight and narrow path, as if they were in danger of falling off a cliff. Nothing goes just right for him, and so he's always angry and squeezes harder until everyone runs away to find some space to breathe."

Leif looked off in the distance.

"I often wonder why Pa is the way he is. Why is he angry so much?"

"I don't know. It's like he is his own worst enemy."

"Well, I hate to say it, but sometimes I think Pa is my worst enemy, too."

They were silent for a while.

"The Woodhouses' church has some teachings about enemies."

"Ya?"

"This is what I remember from the children's lessons: 'When you are in conflict with someone, try to enter into Meeting with him.'"

"What does that mean?"

"I think it means to hold silence with him and be very still inside."

"That is strange, all right. Who would stand for that? Then what?" It struck Leif that, on the other hand, Pa was all about silence. But his kind of silence was as heavy as a brooding thundercloud.

"The second step is, 'Identify with the person.'"

"You mean I should pretend I am Pa?"

"I believe it means to think about his truth, what is true for him. Or maybe it means to know that there is a truth for him, and it will come to you."

Leif shook his head slowly.

"I don't know what to make of that."

"Maybe the meaning of it will come clear at the time. The third step might throw a little light on it: 'Hold yourself open to the power of the truth, whatever it is.'" Leif squinted off into the distance, grimacing as if he'd just eaten a handful of tart pin cherries.

"Go on, then," he said.

"The last step is, 'Allow yourself to feel tenderness toward his concerns and to care for him.'" Leif shifted himself and put his head in his hands.

"I love Pa, but he doesn't make it easy."

"Ya, I know. But I am just telling you what I remember of the teaching."

"Ya, all right."

"Remember that there is a truth for Pa—somewhere deep inside of him—and you are trying to reach for that truth that's alive in him."

"It's very strange." Leif was trembling. Pa must guard this truth with all the force of a boulder gripping its innards. He had noticed how his father's round, high forehead resembled one of the fieldstones that boiled up by the dozens from the earth and often stopped the plow. And when he took thought or was angry, a fierce gash appeared in the stone between his eyes like the crack of doom.

"Leif, remember also that you have had a special experience with Pa, not like the rest of us."

"You mean because of falling out of the wagon?" His scar prickled.

"Ya. You know that Pa was driving the wagon in a drunken rage? We had been at a social after raising a neighbor's barn, and Pa'd gotten tipsy on the ale. He got into an argument over politics and . . ."

"I never heard this."

". . . he yelled at Ma to get the children and said, 'We're going home.'"

"I never heard this."

"So he whipped up the horses and drove off like the Apocalypse. We kids were crouched down in the wagon crying. Ma was hanging on to you and her seat for dear life. We'd gotten a mile away when the wagon hit a hole and out you went. It was a miracle you weren't killed outright."

"I don't remember it—none of it." Leif stretched himself out prone on the ground, pressing his face into his hands.

"It's no wonder. You were out cold." Ellen pressed her fingers into her skull and then sat up with her eyes closed, as if listening to a faint, faraway sound. "After that calamity, Pa treated you with special care, and you have always been different. You have always spoken your mind honestly. I believe that if anyone can reach Pa, it is you."

"I don't know. Pa is angry with me all the time now."

"I don't know either. I don't know why I told you this. It just came up when you said Pa might be your worst enemy."

"It's good," Leif said, sitting up, "but maybe we should get going again." The idea of reaching into Pa's soul sent shivers up his spine.

"All right, then." Ellen pulled some grass out of Leif's hair. Leif rose and removed the horses' feed bags, whistled for Belka, and they got on the wagon and drove toward the farm.

Leif sat on the wagon seat holding the reins, looking straight ahead at the winding lane, sometimes turning out of the track to avoid deep ruts, while the wagon box rocked on its squeaky springs. He glanced at Ellen, who sat looking straight ahead as well, with a sober face. It wasn't like Ellen to be still for long, not talking and laughing.

Suddenly Leif burst out singing: "Oh, Susanna, don't you cry for me! I'm going to California with my wash pan on my knee." Ellen looked at Leif with surprise and glee and joined him. "It rained all night the day I left, the weather it was dry. The sun so hot I froze to death, o brothers don't you cry."

They sang folk songs, chanteys, and hymns for the next two hours until they reached home. Leif was singing "Captain Jinks of the Horse Marines" as they pulled into the farmyard.

The four of them sat down to a dinner of fried chicken, fresh garden greens, boiled potatoes with gravy, and strawberry-rhubarb pie for dessert.

After pie and coffee, Pa went out on the porch. Ellen followed him. When Leif reached the porch a few moments later, Ellen and Pa were walking toward the barn. Ellen was talking. They were similar in build, although Ellen was smaller. Despite Pa's bad knees, they even walked alike. Ellen was, after all, Pa's firstborn, his eldest child. But what different people they were. Leif followed them to the barn.

They all went out to the goat pen. Leif perched on the top rail of the fence, and Ellen went in to pet the dam, Lucia. Pa leaned against a post. "What handsome kids you have, Lucia," cooed Ellen. One of the little ones came around to Ellen's side, and she picked him up, turning toward Lucia. Lucia licked the kid's face and gave Ellen's hand a lick as well. She laughed with pleasure.

"He's strong and healthy," she said. "Ma's tailor money paid off, eh, Pa?"

"Eh," said Pa.

"Ya, it was a gamble. But you gotta admit that Ma's got a good eye for goats!" Ellen chuckled as she turned back to the dam and set the kid down. He went right back to the teat. "She'll get plenty of milk from this one." Pa leaned on the fence rail and spat brown juice between his feet. Seemed he didn't know quite what to make of Ellen.

Ellen spent her days visiting old haunts, picking strawberries, and talking with Ma, Pa, Leif, and any neighbor or peddler who showed up. Her laughter rang across the farmyard like a bell.

When the morning of her departure arrived, so did a pelting rain. Leif backed the wagon into the barn, put the hoops on, and stretched the canvas cover over them. He and Ellen would ride inside under the cover. He hitched up Maggie and Star and drove up close to the porch.

Once Ellen had said her good-byes, she climbed aboard, and they moved off down the wagon trail. The day was wet but warm. The rain drummed evenly on the canvas cover. Leif leaned out now and then to check the ground for potholes and washouts. This kind of fine watering would do the crops some good. After two or three hours the sky grew lighter and the rain thinned away.

"Why don't we peel back the canvas and get some air?" Ellen suggested, shaking her hair free. Like Leif's, her hair got curlier in high humidity.

"Ya, let's try it. We can always put it back again." Leif stopped the wagon and folded the canvas back to the hoop behind the seat. "If only we had a half a day to spare, we could stop by Anna's place and visit," he said.

"Ya, I would like to meet her, Leif. She sounds like a good match for you."

Leif's face warmed.

They camped again at the same site on the North Two River. When they reached the station in Albany the next morning, Leif pulled the horses up and rested the reins. They sat silently side by side. "Ellen," said Leif, "I am glad you came. It was good to talk. You listen, and you understand." He could not speak further. Ellen adjusted her hat. She looked down at the horses.

"Ah, brother, you have a good heart. You are an excellent, honest, hardworking man. Remember, when Pa complains about you, it isn't really about you. It's about him. You will see." She looked sideways at him and gave him a wink. He smiled half at her and half at what she had said.

Leif helped Ellen down, carried her bags to the waiting bench, and gave her a hearty hug. "I'll go now and try to get home tonight. It's a full moon if the sky stays clear."

"It's a full moon regardless, my dear. Don't go to sleep and fall off the wagon."

"Ha! All right, sister."

"Come visit me."

"Ya, I will."

Leif rode away on the wagon. And how would he get to Minneapolis? By train. He could just imagine what Pa would say to that.

CHAPTER 16

Leif Gets Fed Up, July 1881

By mid-July the wheat and corn were growing high. The wheat billowed green in the fields, and the heads were full, promising a good harvest. The corn was tasseled and up to Leif's shoulders; each stalk sported two or three fat ears.

Carrying the shotgun, Leif walked down a furrow in the middle of the field. He spotted a skunk with three or four young ones and trotted back the way he'd come until he was out of range. That's what he got for walking through a field with the breeze at his back—couldn't smell the stinkers in front of him.

He hadn't come out here to hunt. He was walking off his anger. Pa had just laid into him again for working on his shay. He'd unloaded it under a large oak tree near the aspen grove where the old sod hut had stood. He hadn't wanted to leave it sitting under Pa's nose. That would've been just asking for trouble.

On Sundays only necessary work was done around the farm, like feeding the animals and milking the cows. Leif spent all the time he could find to work on the little two-person buggy. How grand it would be to ride into Anna's yard in the sporting shay.

The main tasks were making a new wheel and repairing the axle. The canopy needed repair, too, but that could wait. The wheel was going to be a piece of work. He spent hours studying the shay's good wheel and the wheels on the grain wagon to figure out how to make one. The hub was complicated. There was no way around it: he was going to have to use Pa's lathe, wheel bench, and other tools. And he'd have to get Pa to share his know-how. That was bound to be a sticking point, because when it came to the shay, Pa and Leif did not see eye to eye. Pa thought the shay was a piece of useless falderal, a fool's toy, nothing of value for getting real work done.

Leif saved himself the biggest part of the headache, however, when he realized that the hub might still be salvaged from the broken wheel. He rode out to the Hilgendorf site and found the ruined wheel. The hub was good, and so were several spokes. But the steel tire band that went around the wooden wheel and held it in a round whole was hopelessly mangled.

Pa did a fair amount of repair work for other farmers, so he was often gone for a day, and Leif made good progress. But the time came when he had to assemble his new wheel on the wheel bench, and that was when Pa happened to walk in. Leif didn't look up, but he could feel Pa's eyes boring into him.

"What did I tell you? Why are you wasting time on that wreck? There is work to be done, boy!"

Without a word, Leif removed the wheel from the bench and walked out past Pa. He set the wheel by the shay, grabbed the shotgun from the house, and headed into the cornfield.

The devil. His patience was near the breaking point. Leif kicked a clod of dirt and a pheasant flew up. He shot. *Bang!* Missed. It was Sunday. He had a right to take time for himself, to work on his buggy. Pa himself spent a great deal of time brewing his whisky and beer—and drinking it. Last week Leif had had to redo some of Pa's harness repairs, and of course he had to hide the fact from Pa. Now that his brothers had left, all their work fell on him. He even helped Ma with her work, and he didn't complain. It wasn't fair for Pa to stop him from restoring his shay on a Sunday, when he worked so hard six days a week.

"Come visit me sometime," Ellen had said. He was ready. He'd take Star and leave her at a livery stable in Albany, ride the train into the city. He'd seen how it was done. First he'd stop by and see Anna. Then he'd head for Albany. His first train ride. The notion sent shivers running up his spine.

Leif strode back down between the rows of corn, came out at the windrow at the edge of the field, and turned right toward the creek. Of course Pa would say no. He needn't ask. And he couldn't ask Ma to conspire against Pa. No, he would just go.

He sat down on a big willow limb that hung over the creek, a place he had spent many hours dreaming and thinking since his earliest years. Countless times he had crawled out to the fork and lain looking down into the water. Sometimes he would stare at his reflection until a breeze rippled his face to butterflies. A shaft of light might turn the water gold. The underwater weeds waved like a wild man's shaggy hair.

He'd stow his traveling bag under the bed and stash things he could eat on the way— apples, jerky, hardtack. He'd leave in the middle of the night. Leif stripped the leaves off a hanging frond and dropped them into the creek, where they floated downstream. Hmm. If he took a rowboat down the creek to the Elmdale River, he could make his way to the Mississippi and on to the city. He could eat fish on the way. . . .

The river route would be cheap—no ticket required. But it would take a lot longer than the train. And he'd have to come back rowing against the current. A week or two just now wouldn't hurt Pa any to speak of. Too early to harvest, too early to hay. Ma'd miss his help berry picking. Pa'd talked about topping the corn, cutting off the tassels, but Leif had heard other farmers doubting it did any good. Pa could get a neighbor boy to help if he wanted it done that badly.

The idea took shape in his mind.

A hundred miles by train, Ellen had said. The tracks were a lot straighter than the river—no doubt about that. If he made twenty miles a day going down the river, it might take a whole week just to get to the city. And coming back it would be upriver, against the current. Besides, riding on the train was worth ten carnivals. The *train*. He remembered the pulsing sound in the rail when he'd gone to pick up Ellen. The massive engine, the huge wheels.

By selling hides Leif had saved enough money to cover his fare and a little extra. Peddlers traveling with horse and wagon sometimes bought hides, though they were reluctant to pay cash. They always wanted to give him a cheap harmonica or a mirror in a fancy frame. He'd have to start walking away with the hides before they'd call him back. "All right, I'll give you a buck and a half," they'd say. The train. The big city. He scrambled off the willow limb, grabbed the shotgun, and headed for the house.

During the next two days Leif quietly gathered a bundle of food and a few extra clothes. He packed his rain slicker in the bottom of the bag. He'd take his felt hat in case it did rain. He'd never had to think about packing for a trip away from home before. It was all up to him; he couldn't ask Ma any questions. He borrowed a needle and some thread from Ma's darning box and took a candle and a small bar of soap from the pantry. Tin cup might come in handy. His comb. He laid in his old copy of *Robinson Crusoe*. He hefted *Twenty Thousand Leagues Under the Sea*. No, too heavy. He threw in a copy of *Popular Science Monthly* that he had taken in trade for hides and also packed his record book in case he wanted to write. Nib pen and bottle of ink. He twisted the cork in the ink bottle extra tight. On second thought, he added the Jules Verne book anyway. Might be able to do some trading.

On the evening of Leif's escape, Pa had gone off to bed, and Leif sat at the table reading past issues of the *Little Falls Daily Transcript* by the light of a kerosene lamp. Little Falls lay on the Mississippi River thirty miles northwest of Upsala and was the largest town closer than St. Cloud. He fanned himself with a magazine. "Ma, I'm going to Little Falls to buy a peach from California."

"Oh, who's got those?"

"Grocer named Simmons. I can't even remember what a peach looks like."

"Probably don't look too good, Leif, after traveling all the way from California." Ma cut a thread with her teeth and lay her sewing down on her darning box. "Who needs peaches from California when the countryside is full of raspberries, wild plums, strawberries, and pin cherries?"

"You got me there, Ma," said Leif.

"Probably find plenty of peaches in Minneapolis," Ma said. She let out a sigh while Leif's ears burned. "Can't keep my eyes open any more, son. Sweet dreams."

"'Night, Ma." The blood pounded in Leif's ears as Ma closed the bedroom door. She'd said Minneapolis. But there was no reason for her to suspect . . . Maybe she was thinking of Ellen. He had long suspected Ma could read his mind, but he would still write her a note.

Too soon to leave quite yet. He went back to reading an editorial in the Little Falls newspaper that favored women's right to vote. Leif agreed. He remembered what Ellen had said about Mrs. Woodhouse. Surely the women he knew best, Ma and Ellen, ought to be able to vote. And Anna, of course. They could think as well as any man. Better than most, as a matter of fact. Of course, there was that Scrimshaw girl. She was almost grown up and hadn't learned her letters. But that didn't have anything to do with her being female. Old man Opdahl couldn't read or write either and shook so bad, he couldn't hold a pencil. Sure, females had their weaknesses, but so did men. Fair is fair.

Whenever he saw people unfairly treated, he felt offended. He wanted to set it right. He did not like arbitrary authority in any form or shape. Pa seemed of a similar mind when he complained of the railroad barons and the bankers. Yet Pa did not seem to recognize his own unfair treatment of Leif. This disturbed Leif greatly.

The bedroom door opened a crack, and Leif jerked his head up. Ma looked out at him for a couple seconds and said with the barest hint of a smile, "Don't burn that oil all night, dear."

"All right, Ma." To tell the truth, he couldn't wait to blow out the flame, walk to the barn, and saddle up Star. He'd already taken his bag and bedroll out. Now he was so sure that Ma knew, he didn't intend to wait long enough for her to fall asleep.

Leif pulled the note out of his pocket and set the salt dish on it. He didn't know quite how to word it because he wasn't sure when or whether he'd return. So he kept it simple.

Ma and Pa,
    I've gone to Minneapolis. I will leave Star
at the livery in Albany.
Love, Leif

He puffed out the lamp. In the barn Belka wagged his tail and danced as Leif saddled Star. He commanded Belka to stay, led the horse out the rear of the barn, shut the doors, and set off for the Sederstrom farm.

At this time in the summer, daylight still lasted well past bedtime, and Leif rode smartly along to take full advantage. When he'd gotten out of sight and sound of the farmhouse and no thunderbolts had struck, he relaxed. He was on his way.

Sure, Pa would be furious. But he was angry most of the time anyway, and just now Leif didn't care.

As dusk waned, a bright moon rose, and he let Star pick her way at her own pace. No hurry. In the thickest woods where the moon barely shone through, he couldn't tell oaks from elms. The trees towered over him like imperious elders, and he named that stretch the Wood of Dark Authorities. He picked his way along carefully. Sometimes an owl cleared its throat as if to warn him to stay on the right path.

Star grew skittish as horses naturally will, because they have a great fear of stepping into a hole in the dark and breaking a leg. So he walked and led her by the halter, soothing her with calm words. Some places were so dark that if he had not known the way as well as he did, he might have stopped and bedded down until dawn.

The breath of the ancient trees seemed to come from deep in the ground, and Leif turned up the collar of his buckskin jacket. Far off, a coyote howled. The night air carried sound farther the more it cooled.

Hours later when he reached the willow tree by Anna's lake, early dawn had revealed a world of fog. The moon was gone.

Might be a little too early to ride up to the house. Leif loosened the cinches on Star's saddle. Wrapped up in his blanket, Leif sat down against a tree. He listened to the lake lapping on the shore and waited until the sun was about to rise. Then he washed his face in the lake, combed his hair, and put his summer cap back on. He cinched up the saddle and rode around the south shore of the lake.

When Leif entered the Sederstroms' farmyard, Mr. Sederstrom was carrying two pails of milk toward the house. "*Goddag, Herr Sederstrom,*" Leif called.

"*Goddag,* Leif!"

Anna stepped out the door onto the porch. "Leif! What brings you here this morning?"

"I'm on my way to Albany to catch the train to Minneapolis."

"I'm afraid you are lost, Leif," said Mr. Sederstrom with a look of concern. "This isn't the way to Albany." He grinned. Leif got down from his horse. Anna walked up, and Mr. Sederstrom bolted for the door with the milk pails. "I'm not looking!" he said.

Leif took Anna's hand and gave it a kiss. His color deepened.

"Minneapolis?" she said.

"To visit Ellen. And get away from Pa for a while."

Anna looked down, shook her head, then gave him a searching look. "And you've been working so long to make peace. Sorry to hear that. But you'll see Ellen again."

"Ya, I'll visit Ellen."

"You can't have slept much."

"No. Didn't even go to bed. Read until I left."

"You must be tired."

"I'll ride the train. Come along?" Leif gave her a shy grin.

"Can't. My brother's getting married, remember? Wait, I

have to ride to Albany to pick up the ring." She ran inside while Leif stood with Star. The roosters were crowing and strutting, and butterflies dodged about the sunflowers and morning glories that surrounded the porch. Anna stepped back out looking glum.

"Ma says Lars and Olga's ring won't be ready until Monday, so I'll have to wait. What are you going to do with your horse?" Leif shifted uncomfortably.

"Leave her at a livery stable in town." It wasn't a good solution, but he had no choice.

"Roy's Hotel has a barn and hostler. When I go for the ring, I could bring her back here with me, and we'll keep her. Come, I'll ask Papa."

"Then you'd have to make a special trip to bring her back to town," said Leif, "and I don't know just when I'll return."

Mr. Sederstrom spoke from the porch. "If you don't know when you'll return, it may be best if Anna just took your horse home," said Mr. Sederstrom. "She can bring Gretel along on a lead rope and ride her back."

"You would do that?"

Anna and her father nodded and smiled.

"*Tack så mycket*," said Leif. "You are very kind." He would make sure he returned the favor as soon as he could.

"Why don't you come in and get some breakfast now, Leif, so you can be on your way?" called Mrs. Sederstrom from the porch.

"Sorry, Mrs. Sederstrom. The train leaves at ten o'clock. I've got to be off."

"Hold on, then." Mrs. Sederstrom rushed inside. She was back out in three minutes flat, handing Leif a bundle of butter-and-sugar *lefsa* rolls.

• • •

Leif was soon riding toward Albany, but he wasn't singing. He was concerned about the way Anna had looked at him. She had seemed troubled when he mentioned his problems with Pa.

Anna had walked with him to the shore of the lake.

"My pa isn't like yours, Anna," he had said. "My pa thinks I'm lazy and don't care about farming. He accuses me of having no respect for proper authority and says that I will come to a bad end. But *he* is the one who has no respect for *me*. He doesn't see what I do. He picks out the smallest things to complain about. Then I hear about it all day." Leif was just warming up.

"He never says, 'You did a good job sharpening the scythe.' He never says, 'That's a good job you did repairing that harness.' He never says, 'Nice work plowing the rows so straight, son.' No. He says, 'All you care about is yourself. You waste time writing letters instead of doing your work. You go off anytime you feel like it to see your little sweet muffin, and to hell with the chores.'"

Leif turned and beheld Anna. She had shrunk back, looking stricken.

"Sorry, Anna. I got on a rant." He took her hands. Her arms were limp, and her eyes were glazed. He kissed her, but she hardly kissed him in return. "I'll see you when I get back." His stomach coiled up tight as he watched Anna walking slowly back to the house.

He crossed the North Two River on the rebuilt Olds Bridge without much feeling in his body. Star's hooves resounded on the thick oak planks. At least he didn't have to detour upriver to the Peterson Bridge.

He began to feel awful panic. He wanted to turn back and explain to her, but he had to hurry to meet the train. Leif took Star up to a trot, then a canter. He rode fast for ten minutes, then at a trot for ten minutes. He'd walk her for fifteen minutes and repeat the paces.

Staying on the farm with Pa sometimes seemed impossible. But if he left, his dream of marrying Anna might be impossible, too. All they had talked of was a country life. Now it looked like Anna was backing off—all because of Pa.

Maybe they could start out in Freeport, save their money, and buy their own farm. And if Mr. Fischer would hire him, maybe someone in the city would hire him, too. But it wasn't easy fitting Anna into those pictures. Suddenly Leif awoke to the fact that Star had stopped in her tracks. Her ears swiveled as if she were trying to catch Leif's thoughts. Leif clucked her back to a canter. "Let's go, girl. We've got to make a train."

When he arrived in Albany four hours later, he went straight to Roy's Hotel, where he left Star with the hostler. Then he rushed to the depot, for the train was already arriving from the west, bound for Minneapolis.

CHAPTER 17

The Train

Leif ran for the passenger car where the trainman motioned for him to board. He held out his ticket, but the conductor waved him in. Leif climbed up the steps and into the car, found an empty seat on the left side, and sat down next to a window, bag and bedroll beside him.

No sooner had his heartbeat settled down than the train jerked and squealed, moved ever so slowly for the length of two or three cars, then stopped and sat absolutely still. Leif looked cautiously around at the other passengers, and some curiously eyed him. He glanced out the window, then around the car. Excited children chirped and prattled, crawled and bawled. Some parents soothed and some threatened.

Leif wondered why he'd had to rush to get on the train when now it sat motionless. The conductor came down the aisle looking for tickets. Remembering the friendly stationmaster he'd met when he came to pick up Ellen, Leif asked, "Is there a cow on the tracks, sir?"

"Ah no, just taking on firewood and water for the engine is all."

At last the train banged and jerked, squealed and squawked, and moved slowly, slowly, then a very little faster, and finally a slight breeze came in the window along with the woodsmoke.

The great engine chuffed, and the wheels clacked on the rails. They were rolling. It was ten minutes after ten o'clock.

The train picked up speed, and the countryside rolled past the window. Leif stuck his head outside, and his hair fluttered in the smoky breeze. A cinder struck his right cheek; he quickly pulled back inside. If only Anna could have come. Of course, that couldn't happen unless they were married—or running away. Anna didn't seem inclined to run away.

The steam whistle blew, and soon they passed a road where a grain wagon and team of horses waited to cross the tracks. The people waved, and folks in the train car waved back.

As the train rolled down the tracks, people shut the windows against the sparks and smoke and later opened them again for the breeze. They had to be going faster than a horse could run. It was hard to believe: here he was, Leif Eliasson, on the train to Minneapolis.

Whooooooo.

The racket was tremendous. Between children screaming, men and women shouting over the clacking and rumbling wheels, and the steam engine churning and chuffing, Leif wondered if he could stand it for six hours. This was, without doubt, the fastest a human being could move. Leif glanced out the window and felt a little sick. He closed his eyes, then stood up and staggered to the door. He crouched down, and gradually his heartbeat came into harmony with the engine. Eventually he felt better and returned to his seat.

In a little while the train seemed to be slowing down, and the cars banged together, stirring up the children again. Yes, the train was slowing. Perhaps a wagon or cow was stuck on the tracks. Oh, it was nothing—just a small town. He saw a sign: Avon. It was only a stop along the way. Leif looked out to see as much of Avon as he could: a little shack for a depot, a couple of other unpainted buildings, and a dog pulling a small boy around by a rope.

A few miles farther along came the village of St. Joseph, and then half an hour later the mythic city of St. Cloud, a place Leif had read of but never seen. When they stopped, the conductor warned passengers that the train would leave again in fifteen minutes. It was hot in the train car, even though it was just a little past eleven o'clock.

Leif stood, stretched, and stepped out the door that he had boarded through. He was tired but very excited, and not a little awed, at this strange new world. Walking toward the depot, he saw canvas sacks being loaded into one of the freight cars and passengers climbing on and off the train.

Only two or three passengers on his car seemed to be leaving, and perhaps twice as many boarded. St. Cloud was certainly big. Instead of one main street, as in Freeport or Albany, there were too many streets to count. Near the station, wagons, buggies, and teams clopped and clattered on the cobblestones and dusty dirt streets. Some were sturdy dray wagons, and some of the buggies were decked out with fancy fringes.

As he walked into the depot, Leif spotted massive oak doors with beveled glass and shiny brass fittings. He pushed through them to the boardwalk and looked across the street. A gentleman wearing a black bowler hat mounted a horse at Hawkins' Livery. An older man came out of the Fat Chance Saloon next door and waved his hat at the gentleman as he rode off down the street.

Several people stood outside Kerrigan's Dry Goods talking; one turned and pushed against the side of a wagon with both arms, and they all laughed. A lady dressed in shiny dark green satin left the group and went into Hesper's Millinery. Leif had no idea what a millinery was. They sure didn't have one in Albany or Upsala. And across the street from the dry goods store stood two stagecoaches painted yellow and red. Overhead a sign read "Swanson Coaches." Well, he'd better get back to the train. Leif returned to his passenger car but paused to take another look around before climbing in.

"*All a-bo-o-o-ard!*" called the conductor at the top his lungs. Leif nearly jumped out of his skin at the shout. He ran up the steps, sat down in his seat, and, seeing a mother with two children who had taken the seat facing him, tipped his cap to them.

Standing still in the sun, the car had grown even warmer. Leif's eyelids were heavy, but he could not take his gaze off the activity around him.

The train pulled away. Woods and farms floated by the window, flies buzzed around the car, and Leif dozed. He woke when he lurched forward with steel brakes squealing and the steam whistle braying. Small wooden buildings came into view. Clear Lake. Leif lifted his cap, ran his fingers through his damp hair, and yawned. From his bag he fished out some jerky and an apple and tore off a chunk of rye bread.

Pa must be fuming like a steam engine himself. Leif chewed his bread. No telling what Pa would do when Leif returned—if he returned. Leif had never done such a bold and defiant thing before. It was like running away—except that he might go back. Maybe. Maybe not. No telling. Well, if Pa didn't treat him better, he would leave. He uncorked his leather canteen and washed the bread down. In his mind's eye, he saw Anna walking away again and felt sick at heart.

The train made its way down the line, stopping in Becker, Big Lake, and Elk River. More people boarded, and a gray-haired lady in a hat with blue feathers asked to sit beside him. "Of course, ma'am," he said, stashing his bedroll and bag underneath the seat. She was dressed pretty high class in a voluminous navy blue dress with frilly fretwork around her collar and lots of pleats in the skirt. He glanced out the window and back. Though she was a slight woman, her clothing filled the seat beside him. She reminded him of the banker's wife in Freeport, though a foot taller. She chatted with the lady sitting across from them. Lord, her getup looks warm. Leif's cap was damp with sweat.

They must be pretty far along on the way to Minneapolis by now. Leif looked around to see if he could spot the conductor. He didn't know for sure how to tell where he should get off. The prospect of arriving in Minneapolis cleared the fog from his head.

As the train chuffed out of the village of Itaska, the gray-headed lady spoke to Leif. "May I ask where you are getting off the train, young man?"

"Ya, St. Anthony Junction. Stationmaster said it was across the river from Minneapolis."

"Oh, that's where I'm getting off, too. It's a good while yet. My son will be waiting to pick me up. Would you mind helping me with my bags?"

"Certainly, ma'am. Be glad to." Good. Now he would know where to get off.

"By the way, I'm Esther James."

"My name is Leif Eliasson," said Leif, shaking her hand.

More than an hour passed as the train click-clacked its way southeast through heavy woods and made more stops in small settlements.

Leif worried whether he would even be able to find Ellen. He patted the envelope in his pocket that held her address.

CHAPTER 18

Minneapolis

First, ordinary wooden houses and shops appeared. Brick
buildings were next. In Albany only the bank was made of
brick. Now Leif saw towering edifices of stone. He had never
seen the like. The engine's steam whistle quavered in hoarse
blasts, long and short, as the train pulled into the heart of the
city and rolled toward a great wooden depot. "St. Anthony," said
the sign. Leif hardly breathed. A mix of fright and awe passed
through his body, like the time he'd ventured out on the lake too
early in the season and the ice cracked.

The train came to a full stop, and the car was filled with
pandemonium. Leif followed Mrs. James and took two pieces of
luggage down to the platform for her.

"Thank you, Leif. It was nice to make your acquaintance."

"Good to meet you, Mrs. James," he said. Then he returned
to the car, grabbed his bedroll and bag, and snaked his way
through the mass of people filling the aisle. He clattered down
the steps to the brick platform and stood looking around, wondering which way to go. Suddenly someone barreled into him,
sent him sprawling, and ripped Leif's bag from his hand. A
figure ran away from him with his shirt fluttering, carrying the
bag under his arm.

"Hey!" Leif yelled and lit off running after him. A thief. A robber. "You—stop!" Leif ran down the platform after the fellow, but people kept stepping in front of him, making him dodge this way and that. The thief gained distance on him when a group of men came out of a tavern and filled the boardwalk in front of him. Leif took to the street, weaved his way around some wagons, and nearly smacked into a horse and rider. When he got back on the boardwalk, the thief was nowhere to be seen. Leif trotted down to the cross street and looked around the corner. Gone. His bag was gone. "The devil!" he shouted. He stood looking around, alarmed and confused. Gone was everything he'd packed except his bedroll. At least he'd kept his wallet and his return ticket in his jacket.

"Some scoundrel got your bag, eh?" said a short man wearing a store clerk's apron. "That's a shame, mate. A dirty, rotten shame." He shook his head and returned to the store on the corner. Leif had seen a policeman at the station, so he walked rapidly back. Spotting the cop, Leif went up to him and said, "Sir, a thief just ripped my bag out of my hand and ran off down the street." Looking down at him calmly, the beefy cop picked his teeth with a matchstick.

"What'd he look like?"

"I don't know. He blew into me, and first thing I know, he's running off with my bag."

"Can't do much without a description."

Leif looked at the cop, who showed not a glimmer of concern. No help. Leif turned around and sat down on a bench to collect his thoughts. He lifted his cap and ran his fingers through his hair. Now he was in a fine pickle.

"Do you have an address you're heading to, Leif?" asked Mrs. James. She was standing nearby with her bags. "My son Willie is waiting in the line to pick me up."

"Yes, ma'am." Leif plucked Ellen's letter out of his shirt pocket and held it up. "It's 924 Russell Street, Minneapolis."

"Oh—there he is." She waved to her son, who clucked up his team and pulled the buggy up to them.

"Whoa." Willie jumped down and embraced his mother. "Hey, Ma!"

"Oh, careful now," she said with a choking laugh, "you'll crush my old bones. Willie, will you drop Leif here off? He's going to 924 Russell. We got acquainted on the train."

"Why of course," Willie boomed. "Hello, Leif. Climb aboard."

Leif heaved Mrs. James's bags under the seat and waited for Willie to help his mother up before climbing up beside her with his bedroll.

It all seemed unreal.

Thieves and robbers running about in broad daylight. Leif had never witnessed the like of such a city before in his life. So many streets. So many buildings and horses and wagons and people milling about. So much noise and dust and commotion. The air was sweltering.

As he settled in beside Willie's mother, she said to him, "Leif, I saw you talking to the policeman. Did something happen?"

"Ya! I stepped off the train, and a thief shoved me down and took my bag."

"He took your bag?"

"Ya, so I chased after him, but he got away."

Willie frowned and rubbed his square chin.

"Let's go take a look," he said. Willie drove the carriage down to the cross street and parked around the corner. "Let's look around. He might have gone through it and thrown it down somewhere." Willie leaped down, and Leif followed. They went into the alley, and Willie searched among the trash barrels. He pulled a canvas bag from one of them.

"Ya, that's it!"

"That's what they do: they go through them looking for a wallet or valuables and then ditch them," said Willie.

They went back to the buggy and got on. As Willie drove off, Leif went through his bag.

"Looks like most of it's still here. I kept my wallet in my jacket, and it looks like he didn't take anything out of the bag. Guess my belongings aren't worth stealing."

"Thank heavens. You're lucky," said Willie's mother.

"Ya, I'll say."

"Thieves these days got high standards, eh?" joked Willie. "He was looking for a watch or jewelry—something he could pawn."

They drove across the river on a great suspension bridge and down several dusty avenues before Willie pulled the horses up. He pointed down the street. "You'll find it just over a few blocks, Leif. Good day."

"Thank you, Willie."

"You're welcome, Leif. Have a good stay."

Leif stepped down with his bedroll and bag and with a nip of panic watched the buggy drive away.

Heart pounding, Leif walked along the edge of the gritty, rutted dirt street and looked for street signs. Wagons and men on horseback passed by. After six blocks, he had not spotted Russell Street. He went back the way he came and stopped at Rousseau Avenue. His heart sank with the thought that Willie had simply heard him wrong. He'd thought Russell was Rousseau.

That was it.

He was lost in a huge, teeming city.

Hot.

Tired.

And hungry.

Leif took off his jacket and wrapped it around his bedroll. He walked slowly back toward the spot where he'd gotten off the buggy. Along the way he noticed a park with some big shade trees. Without a second thought he aimed for the shade and collapsed on the grass under a giant elm. He ate some more bread and jerky and finished with an apple. His eyelids were heavy, so he pulled his cap down over his eyes and relaxed. Rasping cicadas, a barking dog, children shrieking far away . . .

"Dang!" someone nearby said. Leif pushed his cap back, rubbed his eyes. A fellow near his own age was bending over a bicycle. The fellow stood up. "Fiddlesticks." Leif got up and walked over.

"What's happened?" he asked.

"The nut came loose on the rear axle, and—look—half the ball bearings have fallen out," he said. He was wearing a fine suit of clothes and spoke educated English. The bicycle was one known as a "high-wheeler." It had a front wheel about five feet in diameter and a much smaller rear wheel. Leif had read about them in the Little Falls newspaper.

Leif had never owned a bicycle, but he could see that the wheel wouldn't turn freely in that condition. He knew about ball bearings from farm machines he'd run. Last year Pa had fixed a neighbor's hay-mowing machine that had them, and he had helped Pa remove them and repack them with Frazer's Axle Grease.

Leif looked at the bicycle and shook his head.

The fellow picked up the bicycle and tried pushing it along, but it was an awkward task when the rear wheel wouldn't turn at all.

"I suppose you'll have to take it to the shop and get some more bearings put in," said Leif. "Look, we could make an easier job of moving it along if I hold the rear wheel up while we push it."

"Yes, that would work," said the young man. "Would you do that?"

"Sure, why not? I'm not where I want to be, so I might as well go somewhere else."

"Well, you're a fellow. My name is Ezra. Friends call me Pitch."

"Leif." They shook hands. Pitch was dressed pretty well to be out on a bicycle, but maybe he was going somewhere. They grinned and set to pushing the bicycle.

"Are you . . . visiting?" said Pitch.

"Yes, just got dropped off in the wrong place," said Leif. "Came to see my sister." He felt foolish for being lost, but he was willing to own it. He was, in fact, lost.

"Well, if you can help me get this miserable contraption home, maybe I can help you find her."

"It's a deal." Leif followed as Pitch steered them through the park and around a small lake.

"I only live about six blocks from here," said Pitch. "Where do you come from?"

"About forty miles northwest of St. Cloud," said Leif. Pitch stopped and turned to Leif. Leif set the rear wheel down.

"You don't talk like it," said Pitch.

"What do you mean?" asked Leif.

Pitch leaned slightly forward and glanced upward at Leif. His face was narrow and earnest. He was not an athletic fellow, more of a bookish type.

"You've got a bit of an accent, but . . . but you don't talk like
. . . I mean, you sound like a regular fellow."

Leif laughed.

"You sound like a regular fellow yourself." They both
laughed and shook hands again.

"I saw you had a magazine. What do you read?" asked Pitch.

"I read everything I can get my hands on. Look." Leif slung
his bag to the ground and dug out his two books. "Jules Verne's
Twenty . . ."

"*Twenty Thousand Leagues Under the Sea*," said Pitch.

"Yes, and *Robinson Crusoe*."

"Grand!"

"And I brought an issue of *Popular Science Monthly*."

"I read that, too," said Pitch. "Would you like to visit the
Athenaeum?"

"The what?"

"The Athenaeum. It's a library that's got half the books
under the sun."

"That sounds good. Sure."

"The heat is certainly disagreeable," said Pitch as they
moved on.

"Yes, it sure is. The train car was stifling." Leif found himself picking up Pitch's manner of speaking. Words came to him
that he had only read in books.

They were outside the park now, heading down Nicollet
Street. They trundled along, avoiding the hard ruts and holes
left by hooves and wagon wheels in muddier days.

"We're nearly there. I surely appreciate this."

"Glad to help." After two more blocks they turned into the
carriageway of a stately house.

"Very well, then," said Pitch. "Look, old chap, why don't you take this for your trouble." He held out a dollar bill.

Leif was shocked. It amounted to a day's pay for most people.

"Ah no, Pitch," said Leif. "That's not necessary." Leif felt as if he was talking out of a grammar book. "I'm happy to give you a hand. Besides, you're going to give me directions to my sister's." Where Leif came from, you just helped a guy out, neighbor or traveler. You didn't take pay; you expected him to pass it on.

"Yes. Your sister's. All right, then. You said Russell Street. Just go down to the corner there—that's Ninth Street—and walk one, two . . . six or seven blocks to the right and you'll reach Russell Street. Take a right, and it's in that block."

"All right. Thank you." Blocks. How strange. Houses in the city lay on lots in rows like an endless checkerboard.

"Can you come by tomorrow afternoon about two o'clock? I'll take you to the Athenaeum," said Pitch.

"I will. Two o'clock," said Leif. He waved and started toward Ninth Street. Pitch ran up behind him, jammed something in his back pocket, and ran away with a laugh. Leif turned and grinned at him. He wondered what was the opposite of "robbed."

"See you tomorrow!" called Pitch. After he had turned the corner at Ninth Street, Leif took a look at the dollar bill. Every time he traveled, he seemed to come by a little money. But a whole dollar.

When Leif found 924 Russell Street, his heart leapt. It was Ellen's address. The place was every bit as grandiose as Pitch's. He looked at the ornate oaken front door set into an arch of sculptured stone. Of course he wouldn't knock there. Ellen just *worked* here; it wasn't her home.

He went around to the back porch and knocked on the door. A woman wearing an apron and holding a cast iron skillet appeared behind the bronze screen. It must have been used for popcorn; he could smell it. "I'm Ellen's brother Leif," he said. "Is she here?"

"Ellen took the children to the park. They ought to be back before long for dinner." Her voice was flat and formal. Leif's stomach spoke. He looked around, wondering what to do. He was bone tired.

"Leif. Wake up." Leif felt the rough bark of the ash tree biting into his back as his eyes opened upon Ellen's round face. He sat up. "I only got a minute now, Leif. Marta is helping the children with dinner. You didn't write me you were coming." She kissed him on the forehead, laughing. She set a plate of food down, and they hugged.

"Here is some dinner." She was brisk. "I'll be back as soon as I put the children to bed." She chuckled in her bass fiddle way, delighted that her dear Leif was here, and she hurried back into the house. The way Ellen spoke his name, no bell could ring in heaven more sweetly than her voice. Except Anna's, perhaps. He swallowed hard.

Knowing Leif's appetite, Ellen had loaded the plate high. Leif attacked a thick slice of roast beef, a mound of new potatoes covered in gravy, and a hill of cooked onions and greens running with butter. Soon his plate was clean.

The ash he sat against was thirty feet from the back porch. He didn't remember even walking over and sitting down. He yawned. Another hour and the sun would set. Mosquitoes were already droning in the shade.

Ellen settled Leif in a cot on the screen porch for the night after consulting Mrs. Woodhouse. "I'll talk to you in the morning." She teasingly pinched his cheek as she'd done when he was a little boy.

"Good night, Ellen."

Maybe Ellen would have to work most of the time, and he would roam around the city. Maybe he should find another place to stay while he was here. He couldn't expect the Woodhouses to put him up. Tomorrow he'd find a lake to go swimming in, too. Ah, that would feel good. Get wet, get clean, cool off.

CHAPTER 19

Another World

Leif awoke as dawn broke and kitchen sounds floated from inside. A little boy came to the door and peered at Leif. Leif made a face at him. The boy shrieked, laughing, and ran back inside. He heard sounds of good-natured scolding.

"Who did you see on the porch?" he heard Ellen ask. "That's my brother!"

Ellen stepped out on the porch, chuckling.

"Good morning," she sang. "Here is some coffee. Hotcakes up in a few minutes." She disappeared back inside.

After breakfast, Leif wandered down the street and retraced the route he and Pitch had taken from the park. Ellen would be gone for a few days. The family was riding the steam trolley out to Lake Minnetonka, where the paddle steamer *Hattie* would carry them to their summer cabin. Leif assured Ellen that he had enough money for lodging, though in truth he'd need to take a hobo's berth along the riverbank for a night or two and maybe nap in a park.

Leif found the park. He walked across the grass-covered grounds under large oaks and elms and around the lake. On the far side he noticed a street lined with taverns and hotels. He walked up to a man wearing an apron smeared with black ink who was sweeping the boardwalk in front of Peltoniemi's

Printing and Lithography.

"Good morning, sir," he said. "Anything a fellow can do to earn some lunch money?"

The man eyed him over his spectacles. "You ever worked in a print shop?"

"I've helped out in one." The man gave him half a smile. "I can move paper and deliver handbills. And I could set type, too." Leif had stepped into a print shop in Albany once and asked a lot of questions. He loved to read, and then he'd seen how things got printed. When a big roll of paper threatened to slide off a dolly, he'd helped keep it on.

"Cool your heels for a minute." The man went inside. Leif sat on the edge of the boardwalk.

When the man came back out, he said, "All right, young fellow. I have a job for you. Step inside."

Leif followed him in. "I see you're no stranger to sunshine," the man said. "You a carpenter's helper, a working man?"

"I'm a farmer's son from Upsala, sir. I came to visit my sister."

"Ah, good. We have some handbills that need to be peddled. You heard of Ignatius Donnelly, the Knights of Labor, the Farmers' Alliance?"

"Ya, I heard of . . . "

"This is about a political meeting. Get these out to workingmen—homes, saloons, neighborhoods, outside the mills and factories—you understand?"

"Ya, I . . . "

"You need to do it fast. Don't lag around. Get them out and get gone. Otherwise the boss's goons are liable to thrash you." Mr. Peltoniemi showed Leif one of the handbills.

Leif read the opening line on the flier: "Let workingmen join hands with the farmer . . . "

"Okay, I see." Pa had joined the Grange and the Farmers' Alliance. He complained about those organizations but not as much as he complained about the railroad barons and mill owners.

Leif took five hundred handbills on his first round and came back a few hours later for another five hundred. He got chased out of a couple boardinghouses and a cheap lodginghouse, but no one landed any blows on him. Mr. Peltoniemi gave him thirty-five cents and told him he'd done a good job.

At two o'clock, having practically walked his legs off, he went to meet Pitch.

They walked to the Athenaeum. Leif was astonished at the enormous collection of books and magazines and marveled at the classic building. The boys hit it off, and Pitch invited Leif to a party that evening.

Leif didn't have clothes of the caliber of Pitch's, but his Sunday shirt was in pretty good shape. His jacket was patched at the elbows, but he could drape it over his arm just right and get by. It was too warm to wear it anyway. And his suspenders were new. Ma had made them for him over the winter, and he'd hardly worn them yet.

"What's the party for?" Leif asked.

"It's my friend Axel's birthday. It's at the pavilion across from Nicollet Island on this side," said Pitch. "I'll meet you down there at eight o'clock."

"All right. See you then."

Leif headed back to Peltoniemi's print shop. He peddled another three hundred handbills and for supper stopped at Iggy's Dining Room for a bowl of Hungarian stew. Through the window he watched grimy mill and foundry workers, masons, and carpenters drifting down the boardwalks toward home after their ten- and twelve-hour workdays. He had two hours before he met Pitch at the pavilion and wanted to take a nap somewhere.

The sun had dropped far enough to ease the heat. He was on Marquette. He walked up Washington to Hennepin Avenue and saw the great suspension bridge he'd crossed with Willie and Mrs. James. He then set out across the bridge and stopped midway. "That must be Nicollet Island," he said to himself, looking over the railing. He looked down along the bank and saw the pavilion.

At the Athenaeum he'd seen a breathtaking painting of the rolling sea by Winslow Homer. That's where the Mississippi went. This spreading, brown-backed stream full of rocks and rapids, floating logs and barges and froth wound through woods and plains for hundreds of miles—through whole states—down to the Gulf of Mexico, to the great rolling sea.

Pa and Ma, Ellen, Rollie, and Elias had crossed the Atlantic Ocean when they sailed from Sweden to America. Ellen might remember the sea, but Rollie and Elias would have been too young.

Maybe he could get work on a barge, float downriver to New Orleans. See the Gulf of Mexico. What fun it would be to go with Anna—if she would ever consider such a trip. They would have to marry first, of course. But maybe she was through with him.

He needed to splash some water on his face, change into his Sunday shirt. Maybe on the bank of the river below. Leif walked back to the west bank and found his way down to the pavilion. He walked past it and made his way down to the shore of the big river where a large boulder was perched.

He climbed up and squatted on the rock. He looked across at the island, full of factory buildings and some flats that might have been for the workers. It was his first full day in Minneapolis.

Too bad Ellen had to work. He'd had no idea. But he could see now that he was on his own. Where he would stay tonight, he didn't know.

This party scared him some. He might be out of his element. He felt like an outsider, but Pitch had invited him. Maybe Pitch was an outsider, too, in a different way. He seemed a bit frail and a bookworm.

Leif wandered up the shore, passing under the bridge. He followed the sandy beach until it disappeared where the river had eroded the bank, and then he climbed up and discovered a wagon track. The track led along the high bank, then came down near the shore again where the sandy beach reappeared. People had built fires there.

Leif looked up and down river and saw that the spot where he was standing was fairly secluded. Quickly he shucked his clothes and waded into the water. Even though the river was running low, the current was strong, so he only went in waist deep and stopped. He dunked himself, scrubbed himself with his hands, and crouched in the cool water for a few minutes. He put his clothes back on and sat on a bone-white log near the water's edge. Now some of his sweat at least was on its way to the Gulf of Mexico.

Riding away from the farm had felt good. Riding the train into the city was worth the whole trip. But he didn't know if he felt good now. He'd been robbed. Ellen was gone. Pitch was the only person he knew. He was a pleasant fellow, but his people were not Leif's people. His people hired Leif's people. Those workers who might go to hear Ignatius Donnelly speak were closer to his people. But they were city workers. They were used to seeing strangers in the city. Strangers were nothing special. It wasn't like Fischer's Tavern in Freeport, where he had spent the night.

Leif figured he'd whiled away over an hour now, so he headed back toward the pavilion in the cool evening shade of the shoreline trees. He sat on the boulder waiting.

"Hallo, Leif!" Pitch hailed him from the bridge. Leif looked up into the sunset sky and waved.

In the pavilion were many styles of cooked and pickled pike, trout, catfish, smoked ciscos, and imported oysters. Leif loaded a walleye grilled with lemon and juniper berries onto his plate. He hadn't had any idea there would be such a feed. Though earlier he'd eaten his fill of Hungarian stew, his appetite was whetted anew. He spooned on the wild rice and small potatoes drowned in butter and malt vinegar. He looked across the table at Pitch and smiled. Pitch winked.

"Most of my friends have gone to Lake Minnetonka, but I wouldn't miss Axel's birthday party," said Pitch.

"I can see why," laughed Leif.

Fruits, berries, berry pies, freshly churned ice cream, custards, cookies. Next, like a heartbreak to those who had no room left on their plate, came the grilled meats covered in pungent sauces. He could smell the ginger on the chicken.

Leif sat down in a chair on the elevated deck of the pavilion and enjoyed his plate. The river ran silently below. A breeze kept mosquitoes at bay. Birds chortled and voices sported. Soon his attention was arrested by a young woman sitting down near him.

"Hello. My name is Leif."

"Hello, I'm Claudia. How do you do?"

"Very well, thank you. You have an interesting accent. What country do your people come from?"

"We're Czech." Her eyes were the dark, rich brown of a pine knot, and her hair was raven black. She extended her hand, and her short, tapered fingers gripped his in a quick squeeze. He didn't know any Czechs, but something about Claudia appealed to him. He thought of Mrs. Charbonnier and the lady at Pulaski's in Freeport.

"How do you know Axel?" Leif asked.

"I don't know him at all," said Claudia.

"I don't either," said Leif, laughing. He wondered how Claudia had come to be at the party. "Do you know friends of Axel?"

"I cook for a family that knows his family." That explained her down-to-earth manner. She was forthright; she had a certain confidence. Also an air of mystery. She wasn't exactly spilling her secrets all at once.

The sun dropped low, and the shadows ran deep. Lanterns were lighted. Chaperones seemed to tuck themselves away, and small glasses of champagne and wine were passed about. Everyone sang "For He's a Jolly Good Fellow."

"Would you like to go down to the bonfire on the beach?" Leif asked Claudia, feeling strangely convivial after two small glasses of wine. They went down the stairs partway, and he waited for Claudia to fetch her sweater. Leaf looked toward the fire.

"Oh no. Here comes Sleepy Nichols. Looks half crocked," someone said. Suddenly a beefy fellow was pressing up against Leif, holding a blade that glinted in the lantern light.

"Gettin' frien'ly with Claudia, horse-face?" Sleepy drawled.

"Sleepy!" screamed Claudia from the top of the stairs. "Are you out of your mind?"

Sleepy turned to look up the stairs. Leif bolted down the steps, fell into the gravel at the bottom, got up, and ran into the darkness. Behind him he heard Sleepy thunder down the shuddering stairs. Leif sprinted on, saw the boulder at the river's edge, and ran up the shore under the bridge. Away from the pavilion no light shone except for a few gas lamps high up on the bridgehead, but he remembered the terrain from the few cues he could make out. Sleepy thudded somewhere behind him. Leif heard a big splash and cursing and ran on.

Upstream of the bridge, where the beach disappeared, he stopped and listened. Hearing nothing but muffled voices in the distance, Leif walked up the bank. He was able to find the wagon track in the trees by mere starlight and what smudges of light remained in the northwest sky. He made it to the spur that led to the beach where he'd had a swim earlier.

As Leif felt his way along toward the secluded beach, he noticed the glow of a campfire. He hesitated. Was it a good idea to approach a stranger at a campfire in the dark? He waited, listening. No sounds of anyone following him, just the sounds of frogs and crickets. He would like to share a campfire with someone after a scare like that. Never had anyone pulled a knife on him before.

A harmonica tune—"Turkey in the Straw"—floated from the direction of the campfire. Leif relaxed and walked toward the light. He called from the edge of the darkness, showing himself as he spoke. "Hullo. Hullo, friend. Sounds good. Mind if I join you?"

A young man in a weathered slouch hat looked up and motioned him over, continuing the tune to the end. "H'lo friend. Name's Philemon. Set y'self down. Have a swig." He held out a bottle of wine. To be polite, Leif took the bottle and tipped it up but only enough to wet his lips.

"Oh, go on, man. Take a slug." He pushed the bottle back.

Leif tipped it up again and took a little more. "All right."

The fellow seemed to have put away nearly half the bottle by himself. He went back to playing the harmonica.

Leif thought about his bag and bedroll. He'd stashed them behind a bush at the edge of the bridge. The night was not that cool; he could sleep without his jacket. He'd get his stuff tomorrow. In a few minutes, feeling a strange buzzing sensation, Leif stretched out alongside the fire and fell asleep.

In his dream Leif burrowed into a hollow log, crawling as far in as he could. At the end of the tunnel he found a frightened partridge. The bird had made a nest in his father's beard. It threw its head back, swelled its chest, and beat its wings frantically. Leif flattened himself out, and the partridge exploded from the hollow over Leif's quaking body.

CHAPTER 20

The Party Is Over

When Leif awoke, his hair and his clothes were full of sand. Philemon was pouring some hot liquid from a pot into his mug. "Want some coffee, friend?"

"Sure," Leif said. His tongue was thick, and behind his eyes stabbed an unfamiliar pain. He shook his head to get the sand out, but that hurt, too. Philemon handed him the pot.

"Go ahead. I got all I want," said the riverman. He paused. "You thrashed around some last night."

"Ya?"

"Look like you got the partridge-foot brand on top o' your head."

"Ya. It's a scar." Leif sipped the hot coffee. It was strong and bitter but felt good going down. He and Philemon drank their coffee and said little. Neither of them was a big morning talker. When he was done, Leif stood up, removed his shirt, rolled his pants legs up to his knees, and waded into the river. He dipped his head into the cool water and shook it very gently. The cool water felt good. This must be why Pa was in a bad humor so many mornings.

"Feel better?" asked Philemon.

"Ya," said Leif, pushing his wet hair back. "Thanks for the fire and the music last night."

"I's glad for the company, friend."

• • •

Leif retrieved his bag and bedroll, crossed the bridge back to Washington Avenue, and stopped in Grindell's Cafe on Nicollet. He ordered blueberry pancakes. He poured maple syrup over the melting butter and forked a steaming slice into his mouth. Claudia. She didn't act like somebody with a beau. Hard to imagine how she could be with somebody like Sleepy Nichols.

Not that he should care. After all, he did love Anna.

Whether Anna had set him down for good wasn't clear. He didn't know for sure if it was really over. Leif wolfed down the blueberry pancakes as if they were his last meal and guzzled his coffee. No sooner had they gone down his gullet than his stomach tightened in a knot.

Leif pulled out his record book. With his thumbnail he peeled wood from the tip of his pencil until the lead was exposed. He looked out the window. The blue-and-white gingham curtains reminded him of Anna's mother's kitchen.

Anna disapproved of Leif's father, or she was just being practical and saw that, most likely, Leif wouldn't be able to work with him. So that picture wasn't going to get painted. End of story. Or maybe she had met someone else.

As if he hadn't just met someone else. He felt foolish about being taken with Claudia. Served him right that she was deceitful. She hadn't seemed that way until Sleepy Nichols showed up. He felt somehow dishonorable to be attracted to two girls at the same time. A man really ought to go one way or the other, not shilly-shally and be undecided.

Leif slumped in his chair. Then he leaned forward and held his head in his hands, elbows on the table. How mixed up can a fellow get? Of course, he knew Anna much better than Claudia. She was the one to stick by. But the question was whether she was going to stick by him. Deep gloom settled on Leif.

"Would you care for more coffee, sir?" asked the lady from whom he'd ordered pancakes. The very thought of drinking coffee pierced his already aching belly.

"No, thank you." He didn't look up.

Maybe he would go down to the river, see if he could get a job on the barges, work his way down to the Gulf of Mexico. Just leave it all behind. See the world, find a new life. Maybe sail away on a ship or a balloon. . . .

"Love?" he wrote in his record book. He looked out the window at the dusty street. It wasn't the heat he found rising in his loins when he pressed his face into Anna's neck and pulled her against himself. No, of course not. That was passion; that was animal heat. They both knew that.

No, it was the regard he had for Anna's good sense, good heart, and good mind. She did have her own mind, and she wouldn't shrink before any man. Yet she was kind and funny, too. He smiled to think of her.

Maybe he wasn't good enough for her. That could be it. Maybe having a father like Pa was too low for her.

Then he blocked out the word "love" with a solid layer of lead, afraid someone would see it and laugh at him. On the next line he wrote, "Leif is an idiot." Angrily he tore out the page and crumpled it up. Stupid. Don't waste paper with such rot. His father's angry question echoed in his ears. "Who do you think you are, den?"

"Would you like some more coffee, sir?" asked a new girl. The older lady had disappeared. The girl's eyes were round, earnest. She looked to be eleven or twelve.

"No, thanks. Guess I'm done." Leif paid twenty-five cents for his breakfast and left three cents for a tip. He'd learned about tips at Fischer's Tavern. He walked out on the boardwalk and sat on a bench in the morning shade, looking west.

If he were going to leave the farm, first, he'd come back here and get a job. Save some money and figure things out. He was scared, but he was ready to go on another mission. His mission. His first solo ventures away from the farm had worked out all right. The walk to Freeport, the wagon drive to Albany to pick up Ellen, the horse ride to Albany, and riding the train to Minneapolis. Leif stood up and, slinging his bag over his shoulder and tucking the bedroll under his arm, walked south down the boardwalk. Might as well head off somewhere.

Carriages and wagons clattered by; horses trotted or stood hitched at their posts. People on the boardwalks hurried, lolly-gagged, talked, loaded, and unloaded cargo. Nicollet was a busy street on a Friday morning.

At a shout, Leif looked up. A horse had just broken away from a wagon team. The horse trotted across the street, stepped up on the boardwalk, and—hello!—walked into a dry goods store. Leif started toward the store to see what had happened. When he reached the boardwalk, out came the proprietor, leading the horse by the harness. He turned the horse over to the wagon driver amid general laughter. "Knocked over a barrel of apples. That's all."

Leif walked on. He was agitated. What would he do? He'd figure out his mission and who he thought he was. He headed for a trolley station down the street.

Leif rode the steam trolley southeast down the Milwaukee line, not too far from the river, through patches of prairie, clusters of oaks, scattered marshes, and a few dairy farms. He stepped off at the Minnehaha Falls depot in a wooded area. Walking back toward the creek, he followed a well-used path downstream, figuring the falls must be ahead. Soon a low hiss arose behind the trees. The hiss grew ragged, then rumbled. Leif saw that a rainbow roosted above a chasm. He walked past the waterfall, then turned and looked back.

The white cascade hurtled down fifty feet, pounding into a creamy froth on the rocks below. It roared like a heavy train rolling down the tracks. Sitting against a tree near the precipice, he stared at it, mindless of time. A small river, set deep in its bed, wound through the woods from the west; the land suddenly ended, and the river sailed off into space.

He felt like that river—ungrounded, untracked, unhorsed. A river making its own bed.

He turned away and lay back on the grassy earth, listening to the roar and smelling the humid rock. Ah, let him float away down the river. For Pa would never change.

And Anna. The very thought of her leaving him shook him, turned his mind into a white froth. It was she who had brought into focus his passion to stay on the farm. If he wanted to stick with Anna, he must reckon with Pa. He must. The impossible must become possible.

A breeze began to stir the trees. For the first time he noticed dark mountains of cloud moving in from the west. He rose and walked slowly back toward the depot and boarded the next train going back into the city. Halfway there, large raindrops smacked the windows and quickly built into a downpour. He put his jacket on, turned up the collar, and devoured what was left of his jerky, apples, and bread.

Leif rode the trolley in wind and light rain to a station at 4th and Washington, and suddenly torrents of rain whirled placards, straw, and trash in a dark whirlpool around him. He froze in his seat. No one left the train. Within moments the wind ceased, and a steady shower ensued. Patches of green appeared in the sky. He ran into the station, sat down on a bench, and after a few minutes of looking around, he pulled out his magazine.

When the sun reappeared about seven o'clock, he ventured down the boardwalk and bought some pickled eggs and crackers in a general store. A street vendor sold him two roasted pigeons, and that completed his supper. He sat on the edge of the boardwalk and ate.

From the looks of the sky, more thunderstorms might move through. Might be a good night to look for a cheap room in a lodging house for the night. Narrow cot, flimsy walls, slamming doors—but Leif was too tired to care.

When the family returned from Lake Minnetonka, Ellen had the rest of Sunday off. She and Leif took a picnic basket to Lake of the Isles, rented a boat, and rowed out to the south point of the big island.

"I wish I could have spent more time with you, Leif. Have you enjoyed yourself?" Their fire of wet wood smoked in the sun.

"Oh ya, I sure did. I met a great fellow, just a little younger than I, and he showed me the Athenaeum and invited me to a party."

"No. Tell me."

Leif told Ellen about the Athenaeum and the party, but he left out the part about Claudia and Sleepy Nichols, so as not to alarm her.

"Night before last I slept in a lodging house on Hennepin Avenue, and in the morning, I ate sausage and crackers on the boardwalk and went to Grindell's Cafe for a cup of coffee. I read in the newspaper about a women's horse race. So I went to see it, and the Minnesota woman was thrown from her horse. Can you believe it—the women have to ride in skirts with both legs on one side of the horse. That's just asking for trouble."

"That's terrible. Was she seriously hurt?"

"I read this morning that she's going to be all right. The newspaper said women should be allowed to wear 'forked attire' in races and use a regular saddle. Huh, 'forked attire.' Why don't they just say 'pants'?"

"Maybe they're using forked grammar. You know, a euphemism. So when do you think you'll go back?" She poked the fire with a stick.

"I'm going to take the next train. There's too much happening here in the city. I get dizzy. You don't have time to digest one thing before another comes along. I miss the woods. I need to go back. I think Anna may be having second thoughts about me because of Pa." He looked away. "I don't know what I'm going to do. I need to go back home and think."

"Oh, I'm sorry, Leif. You must be twisted in knots. I wish I knew what to tell you. You're having a rough time, but remember . . . " She stood up. "Remember, Leif, you are a good man. Don't let the voices inside tell you any different."

Leif stood and embraced Ellen. "Thank you, sister." Leif looked at the fierce light in Ellen's face, stood up straight, and managed a crooked smile.

"Write to me, and tell me what happens," said Ellen.

"Ya. All right."

Picking up their basket, Ellen set it in the boat and stepped in. She moved to the rear seat and sat facing forward. Leif pushed the boat out and hopped in, facing Ellen. He grabbed the oars, turned the boat around, and rowed across the still surface of the lake toward the rental dock. He watched the way drops of water fell from the oars and rode on the surface for a moment.

Leif did not look out the window much on the way back to Albany. He thought of Pitch and wished he'd thought to leave him a note thanking him and saying good-bye. As the train rolled on, he imagined a thousand times telling Pa what he needed to tell him. The train pulled in around 3:30 p.m.

He was on foot now. At Solly's Leif picked up some sausage and biscuits for his supper and some peppermints for Anna. He walked toward Anna's lake until it was too dark to follow the wagon track. Then he curled up in his bedroll, wrapping his blanket over his head to keep the mosquitoes away. In the morning he set out again and in early afternoon reached the message tree by Anna's lake. He left a note in the hole.

Thanks so much for returning Star. I had a good trip.
  I will visit soon.
Love to you all,
Leif

He left the bag of peppermints, drummed on the beech tree, and walked on toward home.

Leif passed through the Wood of Dark Authorities and slept on the ground amid the tall grasses. It was good to breathe the honest earth again. He strode into the farmyard at home in midafternoon. As he approached the house, he spied Ma in the garden.

"Hey!" he called. Ma waved. He dropped his bedroll and bag as she walked quickly toward him.

"Did you walk straight from the depot?" she asked as she stood on tiptoe and threw her arms around him.

"Ya, with a stop at Anna's lake to leave a note. Where's Pa?"

"He's in the barn. How was it?"

"It was good. I'll wash up and tell you all about it."

"Mint and chamomile tea is cooling in the well," she called as he set his gear on the porch.

"Ya, that will be good." He went into the barn and looked in the tack room, where he found Pa.

"*Goddag*, Pa."

Pa gave him the fish eye.

"You decided to come back to my house, eh?" muttered Pa.

"Ya. I came back." Pa bent to his task repairing the wheelbarrow and said no more. Leif noticed that Star was there. "It's near suppertime. I could eat a bale of hay." Leif paused a moment, but Pa made no reply. Leif went to the house. Ma poured him a tankard of cool tea.

If Pa had just gotten mad and shouted at him, he'd feel he'd had a proper welcome home. But Pa acted as if he expected nothing from him, as if he'd already given up on him. Leif could have returned from a trip around the world in a Jules Verne balloon an entirely new man. But Pa cared not a whit. Leif slumped under the weight of his father's silence.

CHAPTER 21

Rainstorm, August 1881

"Up an' at 'em!" Pa growled from the bottom of the stairs. "If you live here, you work here." Leif had opened his eyes just seconds earlier. Must have heard Pa's footsteps. They were going to cut hay in the creekside meadow today. The ground there was too uneven and full of gopher holes for a horse-drawn mower, so they would use scythes.

"Ya, I'm up!" He swung his feet over the edge of the bed and sat up, stretching. He rubbed his eyes with the heels of his hands and felt for his clothes on the chair. Faint light shone in the east. Not a cloud blotted the stars. Today would be hot. It was warm now, at least here upstairs. Still, a faint ring circled the moon. That could mean rain. He wondered what Anna would do today.

Yesterday he'd spent hours peening and honing the scythe blades, but this morning his hunger pangs were keener.

"*Goddag!* Four eggs for me, Ma," he said as he stepped off the stair into the kitchen.

"*Hurså?*" Pa said in a challenging tone. Leif looked at him.

"Please."

Leif took his scythe, a whetstone, and a jug of well water with him to the four-acre hay meadow that lay along Crane Creek be-

hind the barn. The whetstone rested in water in a cow-horn hol-
ster that hung from his belt. He wore an old felt hat, as did Pa, for
it would soak up sweat and cool his head. The sweat ring would
rise up the sides during the hot job of cutting hay in August.

They would mow until early afternoon when the sun was
hottest. Then the hay would be raked into rows and allowed to
dry for a few days. When it was ready, it would be forked onto a
horse-drawn skid. They would lay a rope sling down on the skid,
load a layer of hay, throw on another sling, load another pile, and
maybe a third. Then they'd hitch up a couple of horses and take
it to the barn. Leif would walk ahead of the horses to make sure
neither stepped in a gopher hole. In the barn they would hook
each sling onto the pulley rope and hoist it into the loft.

The sun was only beginning to show its red face. The
morning was still cool, and the meadow grasses were damp.
Perfect. Leif tucked his water jug under a willow tree near the
creek bank and started in swinging his scythe in wide, easy
arcs. The cutting spilled forth sweet aromas of the meadow. As
the sun rose and long shadows appeared, insects warmed to the
morning symphony. Fireflies retired and butterflies awoke. The
air filled with the scents and sounds of a summer day.

Leif fell into a rhythm: slicing to the left and swinging back,
slicing to the left and swinging back. His blade floated near the
ground and laid down a swath six feet wide, advancing by a foot at
each stroke. He moved clockwise around the the field, creating
a loose row of cut hay to his left. Cutting away from standing
grass toward already mowed ground, the scythe strokes laid the
stalks in the open, instead of up against unmowed grass.

While every scyther fell into some sort of rhythm, Leif had
seen some achieve the grace of dancers in their mowing.

Every five or ten minutes, Leif would stop, pull out his

stone, and whet the edge of his blade. If he hadn't hit any tough stalks, he could go longer, but woody stems such as mature goldenrod were hard on a blade. He warmed to his work, and sweat soaked his hat and shirt. The early morning was glorious, and the cadence of his scything led him to sing the songs he had sung alongside his mother and brothers, songs that followed the rhythm of their strokes.

Leif liked "The Big Sunflower" because singing it brought Anna to mind. The song began:

> *There is a charm I can't explain, about a girl I've seen.*
> *My heart beats fast when she goes past, in a dark*
> *   dress trimmed in green.*
> *Her eyes are bright as evening stars, so loving and so shy,*
> *And the folks all stop and look around, whenever she goes by.*

Then he sang the chorus:

> *Oh I am as happy as a big sunflower,*
> *That nods and bends in the breezes,*
> *And my heart is light as the winds that blow*
> *The leaves from off the trees-es.*

He remembered mowing with Ellen only once long ago when he was about ten, for she left home soon after he was able to keep up with the rest of the family. Ellen got them to sing in harmony. Only Pa didn't sing. "You don't want to hear my frog croak," he'd say. Leif thought he'd heard him humming once, though.

This morning Pa had sent Leif to begin the mowing alone while Pa helped Ma with the chores. About eight o'clock Pa began scything behind Leif. Because Leif was halfway through his second pass around the field, Pa was directly across the field from him, some hundred yards away. Over the next two hours, they circled the field twice more, and Leif closed the gap until he was only fifty yards behind Pa. Then he slowed and simply kept pace with Pa so that he would not actually catch up with him. Leif knew that catching up with Pa would irritate him and put him in a foul mood.

By ten o'clock they had half the field mowed. Their clothes were filled with chaff and wet with sweat. When he stopped to touch up his blade, Leif was at the crest of the slope and noticed clouds building up in the west. The ring he had seen around the moon when he woke up that morning had told the truth. They were serious-looking clouds. He reckoned it would rain. Better start raking—and soon.

Leif looked over at Pa and honed his blade. He glanced again at the clouds and felt a surge of energy. Of course Pa had seen the clouds. Now they should start raking and loading the hay. But to ask was to invite a sharp response or perhaps silence, which always made Leif feel a fool. Leif's heart fell. Never could he work alongside Pa when Pa had to have it his way, no matter how senseless, just to avoid agreeing with Leif.

In another hour the buildup of clouds could not be ignored. Thunder rumbled in the distance. Without thinking, Leif had speeded up his scything and caught up with Pa. He looked up to see Pa honing the edge of his blade. "Ya, dey're knocking over de chairs upstairs now," he said. Pa must be imagining a bar brawl in heaven.

"Just so the Lord doesn't upend the throne," said Leif.

Pa gave a short bark of a laugh.

"Ya, we don't want heaven's outhouse coming down, do we, boy."

Leif shook his head at his father's rendering of heavenly affairs. He hadn't meant *that* throne.

"Pa, shouldn't we get the hay in the barn before it rains?"

Pa gave no response.

No one knew how long it might lie wet. Seemed better to gather it while they had a chance. Of course, normally it was allowed to dry on the ground a few days before being raked and hauled to the barn. Otherwise it might get moldy, and then it was spoiled. But it wasn't good for it to get rained on, either. Leif was pretty sure of that.

Pa would not talk to him. He treated Leif with silence, as if Leif were a prattling child. The sky grew dark in Leif's mind. He swung his scythe back and forth, but the music was gone.

The sun was hot and the air heavy. Pa kept mowing, and so did Leif. Half an hour later clouds covered the sky. Soon came gusts and raindrops as big as acorns. Lightning and thunder cracked nearby, and they stopped their work. Pa headed for the barn; Leif picked up his water jug from the willow tree and followed, already soaked to the skin with sweat. His socks had holes, and his feet were sore.

In the barn Pa went into the tack room, and Leif sat down on a milking stool near the rear door. He inspected his scythe blade closely, feeling the edge with his thumb, noticing some nicks that needed repair. He had seen that some woody stalks were plastered with sand, and you couldn't help but be striking it with the blade.

The rain came down in droves, as if it had been penned up and finally broke through the gates.

Maybe now was the time. Maybe now. He would talk to Pa. He swallowed.

"Pa.

Pa?"

Leif didn't even know how to start. While he examined the harness, Pa muttered oaths about the rain and his rotten luck with locusts, low grain prices, droughts, floods, bankers, and crooked politicians. Leif shifted on the milking stool, pressing the scythe handle across his lap. Pa did not answer.

How could he bring this up with him? Pa would just laugh. How could Leif say it? No one had said such a thing to his pa in the history of the world. He was such an idiot to think of it. How could he ever live in this world? Pa said he was an idiot. Maybe he *was* an idiot. Maybe that wagon wheel should have finished him off. Instead, it left him an idiot.

Leif let out a deep sigh and cleared his throat.

"Pa, I need to tell you something."

"What, boy? Are you pregnant?"

Leif smiled as the blade of his pa's joke sliced him. He jammed his fingers in his thick dark hair and pressed them against his skull where the scar itched.

"Pa, I can't take it no more." Somehow he would tell his father what he needed. Even if Pa would not listen, Leif would speak.

"What, boy? Speak up." Leif's ears were full of roaring, as if a great waterfall thundered in the barn. He turned on the stool, shaking and holding his head.

"Pa, will you listen to me?" Leif rose to his feet. "Listen to me! I—am—your—SON. I—am—not—a—stone. I—am—not—the—handle—of—an—axe. Listen to me. I am not any longer a boy. I—am—a—MAN."

Pa looked at him with an eyebrow half-cocked and his lips pursed, and Leif looked at him.

"Why won't you talk to me?" Leif's voice lowered slightly,

and he stared at his father's chest. Pa had taken off his hat, and his hair looked like hay sticking out of a scarecrow. He was looking to the side.

"Yes, I know: I am a young man. But I am still a man," he said quietly. There—the gates were open. The words came rushing out. Somewhere downriver there was a sandbar that he and Pa would row to. They'd sit in the boat and watch the clear water ripple over the sand.

"Pa, when you call me 'boy,' I know you mean the boy I was. But Pa, I am no longer a child. Pa, you are a wise man, a very smart man, a good farmer. You can do many things. Why won't you talk to me? Teach me? It cuts me when you call me an idiot. I'm not an idiot. I am your son. Am I, your son Leif, an idiot?" Leif was appalled at this voice coming out of him. He was speaking his own truth. He trembled and stared at his father, who hung there like smoke, lips pursed, eyes half closed.

Pa was silent.

"Why do you push me back and cut me down?" Leif pleaded. He turned away when a sob clutched his chest. His hand went to his scar, and he rubbed it, rubbed his brow, pinched his eyebrows together, wiped his calloused hand across his face. The rain fell all but unheard in the heavy warmth. The air smelled of hay, horse sweat, manure, wet chickens.

Of course Leif's hands had not hardened into the bark-knuckled paws of his father. But hard and tough wasn't the whole truth. Leif got to his feet.

"Of course I am not an idiot," he said. "I am Bjorn Eliasson's SON!"

Silence.

Leif closed his eyes; his arms hung at his sides. More words piled up at the back of his tongue, but his jaw floated behind his teeth, and he swallowed. Within a moment his father's back-hand would come crashing into his face. He relaxed, became as limp as a rag. Already he could smell the blood.

But moment after moment sailed on like the faintest stir of a breeze. He opened to the silence and looked up furtively at his father.

CHAPTER 22

Pa's Story

Leif looked down at the straw on the floor and stepped around the milking stool. Again he looked at Pa.

Pa stared at the harness in his hands, the crease in his brow very deep and the tip of his tongue clamped in his lips, as if it didn't know whether to go in or out.

Moving as if carried by some urgent force not of his own will, Leif stepped closer to his father. Pa stood motionless, his shoulders stooped, in front of the door to the tack room. His lips had gone slack, as if his mind had retreated to somewhere deep below.

"Pa," said Leif slowly, trying to speak to something buried deep down in his father. "The respect that you show the tin peddler and the neighbor's hired man—I would like to have some of that." At least Pa waited until they were out of earshot when he scoffed at them.

Leif was quaking like an aspen tree. But he was speaking the truth, like Ellen had told him. He would like simple respect, like that he'd received from others. When Mr. Fischer at the tavern told him he'd done a good job and offered to hire him, that felt like respect. And Mrs. Charbonnier gave him respect. The stationmaster, Mr. Crawford, spoke to him with kind regard. Anna's pa showed him respect and good humor as well. And

Pitch and Mr. Peltoniemi. They all treated him well. And Ellen positively loved him. Surely he could get respect in this world from his own pa.

Pa was silent, but Leif was used to that. He had said his truth out in the open, and Pa had heard.

"Pa," Leif went on, "what is the respect of strangers worth to me if I don't have respect from you? How can I work alongside you, Pa?"

Pa turned and clapped his hand against a post.

"Ah, boy, you're too thin-skinned!" he snarled. "You'll never make it in this world without a thick hide! I am teaching you how to be a good farmer and a strong man. Don't be such a —"

"—I know, Pa. Don't be such an idiot." Leif put his hand on the post and looked past Pa.

The crack of doom in the middle of Pa's brow threatened to split his darkened face. He turned around and walked into the tack room, where the harnesses and yokes and bridles and belts hung. Suddenly leather thundered against the wall. Leif half expected his father to come out in a grim rage, swinging a fistful of straps. But there was silence. A cork sucked out of a bottle. Leif sank back down on the milking stool.

Curtains of rain pummeled the ground outside the open barn doors and drummed on the roof. Thunder rolled. Pa walked past him, picked up another milking stool, and set it down near Leif. He sat and leaned back, looking off in the distance. Leif sat with his head in his hand, rubbing his scar.

"Pa, were you ever a boy?" Bold question. Even insolent. But he didn't care what he said. The boulder had not yet loosened its grip.

Silence rode for a good spell. Leif remembered to go into the silence. He relaxed. Pa looked off into the corner. Slowly he turned back. Pa spoke quietly. "Do you want to hear about the old country, den?"

Leif looked up. He met his pa's eyes and nodded. "Ya," he said. Pa had never spoken in his presence about the old country except when he said, "Dis is how we did it in de old days," before he slammed a large sledgehammer into a splitting wedge.

"Allow yourself to feel tenderness toward his concerns and to care for him," Ellen had said. Pa never had spoken of Sweden. Why, Leif didn't know. One glance at Pa's face told Leif that the story brought pain, and he guessed that the telling wasn't easy. Pa sat with his elbows on his knees, looking into the straw on the floor.

"My fodder owned yust a little land, yust four acres he got when his pa was too lame to follow de mule, and he divided up what he had. His t'ree brothers got the rest. It wasn't enough to feed the family. Oh, no. He borrowed against de four acres to buy some more. But it was bad years den, and the crops didn't make. He lost his land and had to rent instead. I was but a small boy, den." He spat into the straw next to the post and took a pull from the bottle.

"My modder had to work for other families. Sometimes she brought home the cast-off bones from the other people's butchering or dinner and made soup for us, and sometimes we had to eat bread made with sawdust."

"Sawdust?"

"Oh, ya. The rain didn't come; the grain didn't grow. Sawdust and lichens in the bread and the porridge." Leif looked with large eyes at his father.

"My fodder became a bitter man. He had to go around and wheedle work from other farmers who were once his equals, but now he had to bow and take off his hat to dem. One man lorded it over another in that country." Pa's eyes looked far away as he stared into the past.

"They wouldn't last long around here, eh, Pa?"

Pa nodded slightly toward him without looking up. Leif's heart raced at these revelations. Small wonder Pa had such a bitter streak in him.

"And the state church lorded it over everybody," said Pa. "When I met Birke and we wanted to marry, Pastor Burstav of our parish would not allow it, because Birke's uncle was suspected of belonging to the outlaw Baptists."

Pa took another pull of whisky and bared his teeth.

"Was it true, Pa?"

"Ya."

"What did you and Ma do?" Leif knew they had married and had Ellen, Rollie, and Elias before they came to America. Leif was the only one born in America.

"Birke had to disown her uncle to the pastor and move into my fodder's house with us. We started our married life there, because we could not afford our own place. When Ellen was born, Fodder could not walk good and had to stay home and tend his little garden. I kept on working for other farmers, and oh, some of dem were devils."

"Devils? What do you mean, Pa?"

Pa's lips were twisted with contempt. "Some of dem would as soon kick you in de ribs as look at you, and you had to take it. I learned dat de hard way."

"What happened, Pa?"

Pa pinched his lips together and gestured with the bottle. Leif had never heard such a torrent of words from his father.

"Once I labored all day grubbing out stumps with a pick

and ax. I was stumbling home, hungry and t'irsty as hell. This man would not bring even water to the field for us to drink. He came after me in a wagon and team of horses, shouting at me, and laid his whip to me. I grabbed the whip and pulled him off the wagon, wrapped the whip around his neck, and nearly strangled him."

"Ya . . .?"

"So he sent the sheriff to get me, and I was thrown in jail for a month. Birke and my mother tried to bring me food, but I nearly starved. While I sat in the jail, I decided to come to America."

Leif's mind spun. Suddenly he realized something about his pa.

"In Sweden then, you had to make every grain of wheat count, right, Pa? You had to take care of your animals better than your children and not waste a single scrap, right, Pa? Any little mistake could lead to disaster. Is that how it was, Pa?"

Pa nodded.

"Ya, so. Den Birke's fodder died, and we got a few acres, a few good years, and we saved a little money, borrowed a little money, and we went to America."

Leif saw that when his pa came to America, though Pa had left the old country behind, he had brought it with him. The old country had followed him all the way to Upsala, Minnesota.

"And you and Ma never saw your parents again or your brothers and sisters," Leif whispered. Pa did not look up.

And even though in America Pa started out on a farm forty times the size of his father's farm in Sweden, even though by the standards of the old country of his childhood he was soon a rich man, he continued to live as though life and dignity were about to be jerked from his grasp, as if his children dare not linger in childhood but must learn every art and craft to perfection and quickly build a bridge over the abyss.

Leif was stricken with grief. What an outrage. What a terrible life. No wonder Pa never talked of it.

He reached his hand out to Pa for the bottle. Pa gave it. Leif pulled the cork and took a slug of the strong homemade liquor. As it bathed his tongue, it burned like fire. It scalded like boiled milk. He swallowed quickly. His mouth and throat erupted in flame, and he sucked in a sharp breath. This caused him to cough so hard he almost vomited. Pa burst out laughing. Leif coughed and coughed until his face was wet with tears, and he began laughing along with Pa. And they laughed; they roared; tears streamed over their faces.

At last they stopped, panting, rose to their feet, and tottered around. Leif was besotted with laughing and weeping; Pa the same, and drunk besides. And finally they embraced each other there in the barn. The aroma of Pa's body was nearly as powerful as the whisky, but Leif pressed his face into his father's beard, and the men hugged each other in a death grip for a full three seconds. When they released each other, Leif said, "*Tack*, Pa. I didn't know dat."

"Ya, you are a good man, son," croaked Pa, looking down. Pa stood close to him, and they firmly shook hands, each casting a shy glance at the other. Pa's eyes did not look like ice so much now. Pa and Leif glanced outside as the rain rumbled upon the roof and shined the ground.

Ma appeared in the front barn door wearing an oilcloth slicker. "So then, are you two coming in for lunch, or will you be eating raw eggs and hay?" Her prankish eyes filled with questions as she spoke, looking from one to the other of them.

"Ya, Ma, we be coming, den," said Pa. When she turned to go to the house, a pair of wet partridges walked warily into the back of the barn.

CHAPTER 23

Where There's a Wheel

In the morning Leif rose as the eastern sky took on a ruby glow.

"*Goddag*," said Ma as Leif filled his bowl with steaming oatmeal from the pot on the stove. He sprinkled on some cinnamon.

"*Goddag*, Ma." He carved a slice of butter and dropped it onto the hot mush, poured some maple syrup into it, and then some milk.

"Couple eggs, den?" said Ma.

"Ya, sure. *Tack*," said Leif. "I will go to see Anna today."

"It's a good day, looks like. I fixed you a lunch bag."

"*Tack*," said Leif, giving Ma a nod and a smile. He felt his face flush as he caught her sparkling eyes. "Where's Pa?"

"He's still in bed. Ya, he was up late working in the wagon shed." Leif brushed the top of his head, wondering what call Pa might have found to stay up past his bedtime. He'd have liked to ask Pa's leave to take Star. Then at least he wouldn't be angry about that.

"You can take Star," said Ma. "Pa won't mind."

By the time Leif walked out to saddle up Star, the sun was throwing yellow light across the ground and splashing up the front of the barn. The air was chill, the ground dewy, and the breath of cut meadow grass and damp soil filled his chest. Leif removed the bar from the doors and swung them open wide.

He walked into the barn and beheld an apparition. There stood his shay in the slanting light, wheel made good, all ready to go.

Leif harnessed Star to the shay and climbed into the seat. Horace rose up on his front legs and grunted softly. "It's a new day, my friend," said Leif.

Leif drove as fast as he dared to the Sederstrom farm. What a thrill it was to drive his little two-wheeler. Despite the ruts and stones, the shay seemed to float above the ground. The canopy needed repair; it swayed and squeaked, so he drove with it folded back. The shay rode well enough at a trot as long as he didn't hit any potholes or rocks.

In one stretch he pushed Star into a canter, and one gopher hole was nearly enough to catapult him and the shay into the tall grass. Maybe that's what had broken the wheel and canopy in the first place. He slowed Star back to a walk but took her up to a trot for a spell now and then when the way looked clear.

When he passed through the Wood of Dark Authorities, they seemed to have opened more to the light. He emerged again into the prairie scrub, crossed Crane Creek, and arrived in early afternoon—record time.

Alder Sederstrom walked slowly around the shay, puffing his pipe.

"You know, Leif," he said, "it's snappy. It's not half bad. Do you mind if I take the missus for a spin?"

Leif laughed. "Of course, Mr. Sederstrom. Please, be my guest."

"I'm kidding, Leif."

"No, be my guest."

"Your horse is tired. She needs to rest a bit."

"Ya. Well then, you could hitch up one of yours. . . ." Leif looked toward the porch. Anna stood waiting, shading her eyes with her hand.

"Hey!" he called.

"Are you going to take me for a ride?" she asked.

"Once our elders have had a spin."

"Would you like some peppermint tea?" Anna asked.

Leif stepped out of the shay. Mr. Sederstrom led Star and the shay toward the barn and waved Leif on.

"You go ahead, Leif."

"*Tack*, Mr. Sederstrom." Mr. Sederstrom put Star in the corral next to the barn where she could drink and eat a bit of oats.

Leif turned toward Anna, holding his hat in front of him, and, with his eyes dancing, he said quietly, "That would be ambrosia, my lady, nectar of the gods."

Anna smiled. She wore a Sunday dress, very fetching, with her shining hair done up in coiled braids.

Mrs. Sederstrom set out some leftover fish and potatoes for Leif. He told them how he'd found the shay and how Pa had helped him restore it. Then Mr. and Mrs. Sederstrom harnessed up Frida and took the sporty little buggy down the lane.

"We'll go when they get back," he told Anna with a wink.

They walked along the shore of the lake. Anna said it was called Bluegill Lake. It had a good supply of panfish and bullheads, and a few perch and rock bass, but little else. Its southern shore was shallow, crowded with cattails and lily pads, so they walked along the northern edge to a stand of ancient white pines, where red needles, bleached gold in the sun, made a soft mat on the ground.

Leif laid his jacket down, and they sat and watched the waves lap the shore. They breathed in the dark smell of the lake and the light scent of the pine trees.

"So your pa helped you fix the shay? Things are better then?" asked Anna.

Leif nodded at her, then gazed out toward the lake and heaved a sigh.

"Ya, a rainbow came out. I found the shay fixed just this morning when I went to saddle up Star." Leif kept looking across the water. It was hard to lay it all out.

"We talked in the barn yesterday. We were cutting hay, and it rained."

Anna studied his face.

"Tell me, but only if you want to."

"Ya." He looked steadily out across the shimmering lake while images of the drama in the barn played in front of him.

Little by little, Leif told Anna how it had happened. Anna moved closer and took his hand. Red, blue, and green dragon-flies soared in the sun.

Author's Note

The setting of *Leif's Journey* is based on the central Minnesota farming community of Upsala, the area where my paternal great-grandparents homesteaded after immigrating from Sweden. My chief concern has been to make the historical setting broadly authentic, even if some geographic details, such as place names or spellings, were changed. Upsala, Freeport, Albany, and Little Falls are actual towns in the area. The towns and villages mentioned along the route of Leif's train trip still exist, except for Itaska. Swedish utterances are generally cast in italics, except for 'yes' and 'no.' Those words are used frequently and have Swedish spellings ('ja' and 'nej') that might tend to be mispronounced, so I have treated them as English adoptions and spelled them 'ya' and 'nay.'

Acknowledgements

I will name only a few of my creditors as examples of how much I owe to all. My barber, Pete LeBak, is about seventy-six and grew up in Wyoming where his father farmed with horses. Pete can still name all the parts of the implements and harnesses and spins plenty of yarns about the behavior and merits of oxen, horses, mules, and other farm animals. Pete also knows how to fix the generator in a 1939 Ford truck and can tell you what kinds of shells were fired by a Civil War era Springfield rifle. He is a goldmine of period trivia and never tells a customer the same joke twice. My brother Larry, a lifelong hunter, advised me on how to field dress a deer.

A friend gave me a reservation to spend the night in McCone's Sod House on the Prairie bed-and-breakfast near Walnut Grove, Minnesota, where Laura Ingalls lived. People were also generous with their time and expertise. I consulted therapists, Swedes, amateur and professional historians, and a theatrical clothing specialist. I plundered the physical and electronic troves of the Minnesota Historical Society, the special historical collections of the Hennepin County Library, and the historical societies of Isanti, Morrison, and Hennepin Counties and the city of Upsala, as well as the internet and the memories of assorted elders.

Some twenty men shared intimate stories with me about

their fathers. Many friends read the manuscript at different stages. I'm especially grateful to my writers' group of Jane Resh Thomas alumnae, a motley and prolific crew so long-suffering, they read my manuscript three times. Jan de Hartog's novel *The Peaceable Kingdom* provided a key lesson in conflict management. Finally, I thank that evangelist of compassionate communication, Marshall Rosenberg, for inventing camel ears.

Part of the setting is Minneapolis, and there I tried to stay as faithful as possible to historical names, conditions, and features, although again, some details are fictitious. Because spiritual and psychological dynamics are important to the story, I sought out evidence of how people of that time dealt with the panoply of human emotions. That evidence appeared most often in the diaries and journals of women, who were more likely to write about such matters than were men. I also took for granted that the lexicon of passions and emotions displayed in the Bible would have been part of the culture of the time. The key challenge was to render the conflict negotiated by Leif and his father in period-appropriate terms since they lived long before the era of modern psychotherapy.

Made in the USA
Charleston, SC
02 January 2015